B Is for Beer

Billed by the author as 'the first children's book about beer', this inspired work taps into the barrel of life's existential mysteries and is, of course, truly meant to sit proudly alongside his other novels in the grown-ups literature section

Also by Tom Robbins

Another Roadside Attraction
Even Cowgirls Get the Blues
Still Life with Woodpecker
Jitterbug Perfume
Skinny Legs and All
Half Asleep in Frog Pajamas
Fierce Invalids Home From Hot Climates
Villa Incognito
Wild Ducks Flying Backward

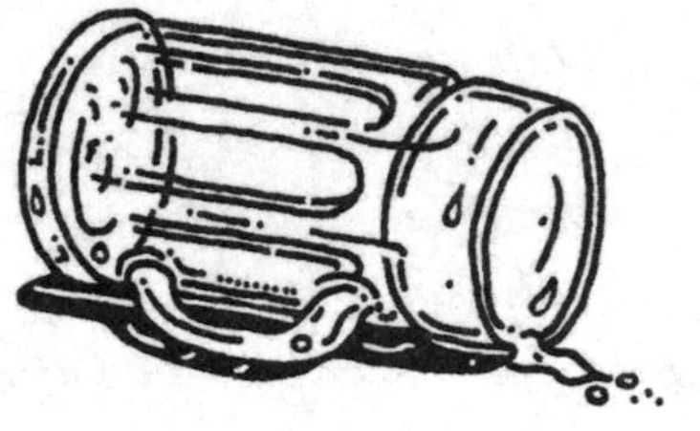

Tom Robbins

NO EXIT PRESS

This edition published in the UK in 2010 by
No Exit Press
P.O.Box 394, Harpenden, Herts, AL5 1XJ
www.noexit.co.uk

Published by arrangement with Ecco,
an imprint of Harper Collins Publishers, New York, USA

A CIP catalogue record for this book is available from the British Library.

This is a work of fiction. Names, characters, places, and incidents either are the product of the author's imagination or are used fictitiously, and any resemblance to actual persons, living or dead, businesses, companies, events or locales is entirely coincidental.

Designed by McSweeney's
Cover and interior art © Les LePere

The first chapter of *B Is for Beer* was originally published in the *Seattle Post-Intelligencer* in May 2007, when Tom Robbins was writer-in-residence at that newspaper.

ISBN 978-1-84243-335-5

2 4 6 8 10 9 7 5 3 1

Printed in Great Britain by JF Print & Co Ltd., Sparkford, Somerset

This one is for Blini.

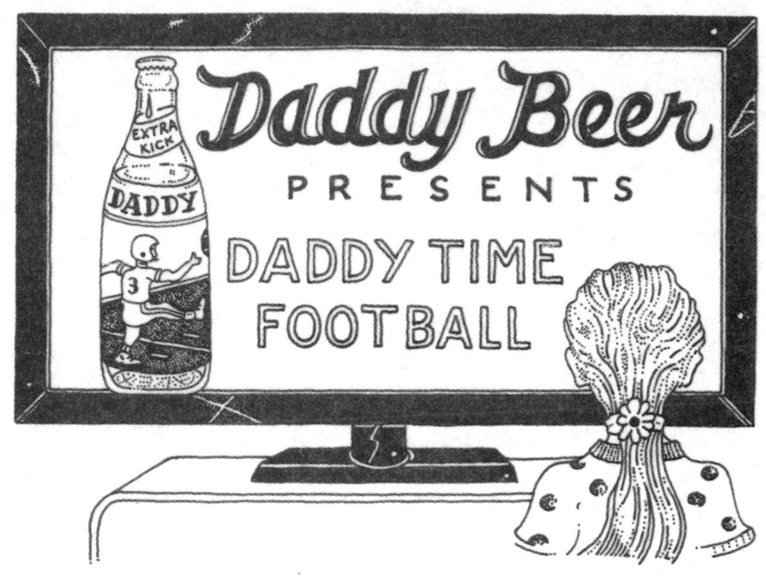

1

Have you ever wondered why your daddy likes beer so much? Have you wondered, before you fall asleep at night, why he sometimes acts kind of "funny" after he's been drinking beer? Maybe you've even wondered where beer comes from, because you're pretty sure it isn't from a cow. Well, Gracie Perkel wondered those same things.

"Mommy," Gracie asked one afternoon, "what's that stuff Daddy drinks?"

"You mean coffee, sweetie?"

"Not coffee. Ick! That other stuff that's yellow and looks like pee-pee."

"Gracie!"

"*You* say pee-pee."

"Well, when I'm talking about potty time I might. But I don't say it about somebody's beverage."

Gracie giggled. Her mother, who was busy loading clothes in the washer, suggested without looking up, "I believe, dear, you're talking about beer."

"Oh!" squealed Gracie. "That's right. *Beer*. That stuff that's always on TV." She deepened her voice. " 'Better tasting!' 'Less filling!' 'Better tasting!' 'Less filling!' " She giggled again. "Is it kinda like Pepsi for silly old men?"

Mrs. Perkel smiled, but it was such a weak, wimpy smile a kitten could have knocked it halfway to Milwaukee. She paused in her work to stare out of the laundry room window. The clouds themselves looked like a big pile of dirty laundry. That was not unusual because, you see, the Perkel family lived in Seattle.

Do you know about drizzle, that thin, soft rain that could be mistaken for a mean case of witch measles? Seattle is the world headquarters of drizzle, and in autumn it leaves a damp gray rash on everything, as though the city were a baby that had been left too long in a wet diaper and then rolled in newspaper. When there is also a biting wind, as there was this day, Seattle people sometimes feel like they're trapped in a bad Chinese restaurant; one of those drafty, cheaply lit places where the waiters are gruff, the noodles soggy, the walls a little too green, and although there's a mysterious poem inside every fortune cookie, tea is invariably spilt on your best sweater. Mrs. Perkel must have been feeling that way, for she sighed at the limp pork dumplings (or were they wadded Pampers?) in the sky and said to Gracie, "If you want to know about beer you should go ask your father."

Never mind that she was wearing fluffy fuzzy bunny slippers, Gracie still tiptoed into the den. Her daddy was watching football on their new flat plasma screen, and if the University of Washington was losing again, he'd be in a grumpy mood. Uh-oh. She overheard a naughty word. UW was losing. Gracie was relieved, however, when she noticed that Uncle Moe had dropped by to watch the game and, of course, to mooch a few beers from her dad.

Uncle Moe didn't take sports very seriously. He called himself a philosopher, if you know what that is. He'd graduated from about a dozen colleges, seldom ever seemed to work, and had traveled just about every place a person could go without getting his head chopped off. Mrs. Perkel said he was a "nut job," but Gracie liked him. It didn't bother her that he had a face like a sinkful of last night's dinner dishes or that his mustache resembled a dead sparrow.

Timidly, Gracie tapped Mr. Perkel on the elbow. Her voice was shy and squeaky when she asked, "Daddy, can I please taste your beer?"

"No way," her father snorted over his shoulder. His eyes never left the screen. "Beer's for grown-ups."

Gracie turned toward Uncle Moe, who grinned and beckoned her over, as she had suspected he might. Uncle Moe extended his can—and just like that, behind her daddy's back, little Gracie Perkel took her first sip of beer.

"Ick!" She made a face. "It's *bitter*."

"The better to quench your thirst, my dear."

"What makes it bitter, Uncle Moe?"

"Well, it's made from hops."

Gracie made another face. "You mean them jumpy bugs that…?"

"No, pumpkin, beer isn't extracted from grasshoppers. Nor hop toads, either. A hop is some funky vegetable that even vegans won't eat. Farmers dry the flowers of this plant and call them 'hops.' I should mention that only the female hop plants are used in making beer, which may be why men are so attracted to it. It's a mating instinct."

"Moe!"

The uncle ignored Gracie's father. "In any event," he went on, "when brewers combine hops with yeast and grain and water, and allow the mixture to ferment—to rot—it magically produces an elixir so gassy with blue-collar cheer, so regal with glints of gold, so titillating with potential mischief, so triumphantly refreshing, that it seizes the soul and thrusts it toward that ethereal plateau where, to paraphrase Baudelaire, all human whimsies float and merge."

"Don't be talking that crap to her. She's five years old."

"Almost six," chimed Gracie.

"In Italy and France, a child Gracie's age could walk into an establishment, order a beer, and be served."

"Yeah, well those people are crazy."

"Perhaps so—but there's far fewer alcohol problems in their countries than in safe and sane America."

Mr. Perkel muttered something vague before focusing his frown on UW's latest boo-boo. Uncle Moe removed another beer from the cooler, holding it up for Gracie to admire. "Beer was invented by the ancient Egyptians," he said.

"The ones who made the mummies?"

"Exactly, although I don't believe there's any connection. At least I hope not. The point is, the Egyptians could have invented lemonade—but they chose to invent beer instead."

While Gracie thought this over, Uncle Moe pulled the metal tab on the top of his beer can. There was a snap, followed by a spritzy hiss and a small discharge of foam. Uncle Moe took a long drink, wiped foam from his tragic mustache, and said, "Speaking of inventions, did you know that the tin can was invented in 1811, but can openers weren't invented until 1855? It's a fact. During the forty-four years in between, hungry citizens had to access their pork 'n' beans with a hammer and chisel. They were pretty lucky, don't you think, that in those days beer didn't come in cans?"

At that moment there was a time-out on the football field and Mr. Perkel got up to go to the bathroom. You yourself may have noticed that beer causes big strong men to piddle like puppies.

"Have you heard of Julia Child, the famous cook? When she moved to Paris in 1948, she brought along a case of American beer. Her French maid had never seen beer in cans before, and she tried to flush the empties down the toilet. Naturally, it overflowed. Took a plumber nearly three days to unclog the pipes."

Gracie laughed. She looked at the empty cans lying around the den, thinking that flushing them down the toilet might be a funny trick to play on her daddy. Or would it? She'd have to think about it some more.

Once again, Uncle Moe passed his beer to Gracie. She hesitated, but being an adventurous little girl, she eventually took another swallow. Although she didn't say "ick," it didn't taste any better than the first time.

"Your pediatrician isn't likely to mention this—unless he's Irish, of course—but beer does have some nutritional value. The Chinese word for beer means 'liquid bread.' " Uncle Moe paused to drink. "Even the most wretched macrobrew contains a six-pack of vitamins: thiamine, riboflavin, pantothenic acid, pyridoxine, biotin, and… oh yes, cyanocobalamin. Can you say cyanocobalamin?"

"Cyno… cyho… cyoballyman… cy…"

"Okay, close enough. Presumably, they're each a member of the vitamin B family but precisely what health benefits those little jawbreakers provide I haven't a clue."

Gracie didn't care what benefits they provided. As far as she was concerned, vitamins were even ickier than beer.

"I'll tell you what," said Uncle Moe, almost in a whisper. "On Monday we'll inform your mother that I'm taking you to Woodland Park. Instead, we'll secretly ride the bus out to the Redhook brewery. We'll go on their tour and you can see for yourself exactly how beer is made. Most educational, my dear, most educational. After the tour, I'll sneak you into the taproom and we'll watch the bartender water the monkeys. It's better than the zoo."

Practically burping with excitement (or was it the beer?), Gracie skipped out of the den. Her birthday was so darn slow in coming she feared she was likely to be a teenager before she could ever turn six, but now she had something right away to look forward to.

2

At Sunday school the next morning, Gracie took a seat in the rear of the classroom. If she could, she always sat toward the back because she had a sensitive nose and the teacher's breath was so bad it could paralyze a rattlesnake. Gracie was not really paying attention, was in fact kind of dozing off, fantasizing about the pink cell phone and the puppy she wanted for her birthday, when she thought she heard the teacher say something about the ancient Egyptians.

Gracie hit the Pause button on her daydream machine and looked up just as the teacher asked, "Why, class, do you suppose that ol' Pharaoh, the king of Egypt, commanded all Israelite boy babies to be drowned in the river?"

Fully awake now, Gracie believed she might have the answer. She raised her hand. "To keep 'em from growing up and drinking all the Egypt's beer," she said brightly.

The teacher gave her a very long, very strange look before going on to answer the question herself, all the while exhaling fumes that would have parted the Red Sea and saved Moses the trouble. Later, out on the church steps, the teacher drew

Mrs. Perkel aside and talked to her in a low voice, directing occasional glances at Gracie.

After Sunday lunch, which Gracie and her mom ate alone, Mr. Perkel being off playing golf with his buddies, she was sent to her room. Jail time. She didn't mind much because she often spent afternoons in her room, listening to music (and sometimes dancing: she had a lot of really great moves in her repertoire), but that day she was troubled by the uneasy feeling that she was going to be more severely punished when her daddy came home from the golf course. (You know what the game of golf is, don't you? It's basketball for people who can't jump and chess for people who can't think.) To make matters worse, she had no idea what she had done wrong.

As it turned out, however, the family drove to Picora's for a pizza early that evening, and not one word was uttered about Gracie's behavior. Maybe the Sunday school teacher's breath had frozen the memory section of Mrs. Perkel's brain.

In any case, Gracie, relieved, fell asleep that night with a secret smile because in the morning she and Uncle Moe were going off on an adventure. And because she wasn't a baby Israelite boy in ancient Egypt.

3

Have you ever felt—or imagined—that there is more than one world? Does it sometimes seem to you that there is the familiar world you wake up in every morning and another world to the right or the left of this one, just out of reach, where interesting things (some wonderful, some rather creepy) are occurring that you can't quite describe or put your finger on: a world where your Hello Kitty ticktock clock refuses to obey rules of time, where mommies and daddies don't work all day; where trees, certain rocks, and maybe even shoes live secret lives of their own? You never talk about this sensation or even think about it too much because it has a fragrance of silliness about it, but once in a great while, such as when you're lying in bed or walking down an exceptionally dark street, doesn't it seem almost too real to be denied?

Well, that famous Seattle drizzle, the ceaseless thin gray rain that we described before, the mist that can soften and even erase the lines that separate one shape from another, that very same penetrating drizzle has the ability to melt the shadow between Our World and the Other World. At least, some people think so, although to be truthful, most of those people are old Indians, hippies, mushroom hunters, or children such as Gracie Perkel.

Monday morning turned out to be especially drizzly, needled with a silent, spidery rain that was almost as thick as fog. Normally, on such a damp, dark day, Gracie might have stared out of her bedroom window, alert for signs of angels, Sasquatch, mossy-haired spooks, magic gods, or half-invisible wild fox spirits. Today, however, she bounced immediately from bed—and you know the reason why.

She padded into the bathroom, splashed water on her face, took what she called a "speed poop" (barely two grunts), and swiped a toothbrush across her gums so quickly it didn't even tickle any bacteria, let alone kill them. Then, still in her jam-jams, she slid down the bannister and skipped to the breakfast table, already tasting the strawberry Pop-Tart on her tongue.

There was really no need to rush around in that manner. Gracie was well aware that Uncle Moe never rolled out of bed before ten a.m. Uncle Moe believed early rising was an unhealthy practice, harmful to both the nerves and the liver. Nevertheless, she was too anxious to dawdle. Recently she'd been a bit bored with her life (her kindergarten was only in session Tuesdays, Wednesdays, and Thursdays), so the prospect of an excursion with the so-called family nut job had thrilled her more than might seem logical.

Brurble-urbel-urbel! Gracie had just lifted a freshly filled milk glass to her lips when the telephone burbled. Mrs. Perkel answered the kitchen wall phone, saying, rather sarcastically, "Well, well, if it isn't the ol' philosopher." There was a pause. Gracie held the milk glass in place without drinking. "Gee, that's too bad," her mom said then, with what struck Gracie as a certain lack of sincerity. "Very sorry to hear that."

The arm that held the milk glass was frozen in place. What could possibly be the matter? No amount of rain would cause Uncle Moe to delay or cancel their plans. To Uncle Moe, who often boasted that he owned neither a slicker nor an umbrella, a rainy day was merely another cause for celebration.

"Okay, I'll give her the sad news," Mrs. Perkel said. She hung up and turned to Gracie. "I'm afraid Moe won't be taking you to the park today, honey. He hurt his foot and has to see a doctor."

"Oh." Gracie set the glass down without having taken a sip. So disappointed was she that she nearly forgot her manners. Finally, after a long moment, she asked in a concerned but faint little voice, "How did he hurt his foot?"

Planting her hands on her hips, Mrs. Perkel shook her head from side to side and smiled. "He dropped a beer can on it," she said.

4

If it is the ambition of every Pop-Tart to be eaten and enjoyed, there was one in the Perkel household that was destined to exist in vain. Gracie left the table without touching a single bite of breakfast. Back to her room she scurried, closed the door, and flopped onto the bed. So deeply did she bury her face in the white pillowcase you might have believed that above the neck she was one of those Egyptian mummies (though of Egypt we should probably say no more). Soon her pillow was as soaked as if it had been left out in the yard.

Do you think she was overreacting? Could her disappointment really have been that horrible? No, Gracie was no crybaby wimp. Furthermore, she was hardly a stranger to disappointment as her daddy was forever—forever! forever!—promising to take her places, to play games with her or buy her things, only to forget about it when the time came. What had upset Gracie, what had gotten her so worked up, was not so much disappointment as it was embarrassment and humiliation.

She was only five (okay, almost six) but she wasn't stupid. She knew that no beer can was heavy enough to injure a grown man's foot by falling on it. Maybe it was her mother, maybe it was Uncle Moe, maybe it was both of them together, but somebody was fibbing in order to shame her. Somebody she loved was making cruel fun of her, undoubtedly because of all that interest she had shown in beer on Saturday; and probably, too, for having mentioned beer during church on Sunday. They were mocking her for that beer business and she didn't exactly know why.

She did know, however, that she wanted nothing to do with beer ever, ever again! Beer could totally disappear from Planet Earth for all she cared. She was through with beer. She hated it. She wished the damn baby-drowning Egyptians had choked on their dumb, icky invention.

Her tearwater finally used up, Gracie rolled over and blew her nose on her pajama sleeve. (Don't pretend you've never done anything similar.) She lay there throughout the morning, uninterested in listening to music, choosing not to watch her *Finding Nemo* video for the thirty-seventh time, and most assuredly not inspired to dance.

Mostly, she just gazed through the drizzle-speckled window at the distant hills, as if expecting, actually longing, to detect otherworldly signs in the mist; signs, for example, of legendary stick Indians, signs of tricksters, phantom outlaws, enchanted dwarves running through the forest in long velvet robes, or, most particularly, runaway orphan girls searching out hollow trees in which they might make homes for themselves. Once or twice, she believed she saw something along those very lines, although she would have hesitated to bet her allowance on it.

Next, she tried imagining what her socks might be saying to one another in the privacy of their dresser drawer, straining hard as if to overhear socky conversation, but, alas, this game failed to amuse her the way it had so many times in the past.

Gracie Perkel had lost her giggle. She'd lost it. Her giggle had deserted her. It had gone far away. And she wasn't sure she'd ever get it back.

"Hello up there!" Her mother was shouting from the bottom of the stairs. "Lunch is ready!" When there was no response, she added, "Grilled cheese sandwich and tomato soup!"

Don't think for a second that Gracie wasn't tempted. Wasn't her tummy as empty as outer space? Wasn't grilled cheese with tomato soup her favorite lunch? Yes, it was, but why should she eat food prepared by a mommy so heartless as to ridicule her only daughter for merely being curious about the unusual drinking habits of adults? Forget about it! No way, José! Gracie would sooner eat poison.

At that moment, she heard a car pull up in the driveway. It was a big yellow taxi. And soon there was the ol' Moester being helped from the vehicle. Uncle Moe in his pinstriped suit, dark glasses, and artistic French beret. He was supporting himself with crutches. On his left foot there was one of those medical boots.

5

"Technically speaking," explained Uncle Moe, "it was not a beer can."

"What was it then?" asked Mrs. Perkel. "Technically speaking." She sounded suspicious, even a trifle irritated.

Moe's eyes were fixed on Gracie with a sympathetic gaze. Although it was past noon, she remained in her pajamas and he understood why. "To be absolutely accurate—and we should always strive for accuracy, shouldn't we, Gracie?—the inanimate object that disabled my lower extremity was not a beer can but, rather, a can of beer. Which is to say, it was a full can. An unopened can. But that's scarcely the worst of it.

"The beer in question happened to be an imported Sapporo beer, which, you may remember, if you've ever seen one in the supermarket, comes in a giant silver container that resembles some kind of Japanese ninja weapon, all tapered and sleek and deadly looking. The Sapporo can holds twenty-two fluid ounces, which is close to a pint and a half, so when one opens one's refrigerator door and a Sapporo unexpectedly tumbles—*Banzai! Kamikaze!*—from the very top shelf and crashes down onto one's bare tootsie…"

"Ooh," oohed Gracie. "Did it hurt?"

"Hell yes, child! It felt like my foot had been run over by your daddy's golf buggy on one of those occasions when it's loaded with lawyers and blondes and a barrel of fried chicken."

Mrs. Perkel moved toward the kitchen. "I've got work to do, Moe. You'll have to excuse me."

"Heaven forbid that I keep any citizen from honest toil," he said. "But before you become engrossed in your domestic labors, would you mind providing me with a little hair of the dog?"

For a moment, Gracie's heart thumped wildly. Somewhere inside her a squeal began loosening its seat belt. Was there—could there possibly be—a *puppy* in the house? After all, her birthday was approaching and she'd been asking for a... But no, her mother instead returned with a cold bottle of Budweiser beer and thrust it at the grateful relative, who, noticing Gracie's confusion, explained then that "hair of the dog" was slang that referred to the practice of drinking in the morning, for healing purposes, a small amount of the alcoholic beverage in which one had over-indulged the previous evening; although in this case the mutt that had bitten Uncle Moe was that hefty can of Sapporo, a can that, as it turned out, had cracked the bone in his big toe and caused him, as he recoiled from the blow, to tear a tendon in his ankle.

"It throbbed like a toothache the rest of the weekend, so first thing today I made an emergency visit to a podiatrist."

If you're unfamiliar with the word *podiatrist*, you're not alone. Fortunately for Gracie (and now for you), Uncle Moe was quick to define *podiatrist* as a doctor who investigates and treats disorders of the feet. A foot specialist. But the ol' Moester, being the ol' Moester, didn't stop there.

"Are you aware," he asked, "that there are more podiatrists in the United States of America than in all the other countries of the world combined? It's true. And my podiatrist says that the reason for this is that Americans lace up and tie their shoes too tight. That's correct. We lace up our shoes and tie them so tight that we end up damaging our feet.

"Now what does that tell you about our underlying national personality? Eh? Any indication there that Americans have a fear of looseness? A craving—hopeless, of course, hee-hee—for security? For stability? Can it partially explain the disturbing tendency on the part of certain of our citizens to huddle together in Wal-Mart parking lots?"

Gracie tried to think about it, but it proved to be a thought her thinker could not think on. When he realized that, concentrate as she might, the little girl was only bewildered by his philosophizing, the Moester took a mighty gulp from the bottle, then offered it to her.

"Beer is at its best when drawn directly from a tapped keg," he said, "but a glass bottle is superior to a can. Cans are more convenient and they're here to stay, but the aluminum's fluctuating temperature does mess with the purity of the flavor." To Gracie's nine thousand eager but inexperienced taste buds, the flavor of the beer from the bottle proved every bit as icky as the flavor from the can, so after one cautiously optimistic swallow she gave the brewski back, sadder Budweiser.

Nodding at the face she made, as well as at the jammies she still wore (pajamas being the official uniform of inertia and depression), Uncle Moe said cheerfully, "The world is a wonderfully unpredictable place, my dear, we're seldom as limited as we think we are, and every cloud has a silver headline. For example, my podiatrist turned out to be an absolutely gorgeous representative of the female sex. I mean, if good looks were two flakes of snow, she could provide nesting grounds for half the Earth's penguins.

"Dr. Proust has straight black hair so long it would take a spider monkey twenty minutes to climb the length of it, she had on a silk dress as red as a terrorism alert, silver sandals, ornate jewelry, and some kind of glittery savage eye shadow, and in general looks more like a gypsy than a surgeon. Maybe it's not surprising that she wants to take a knife to me on Thursday." He grinned. "I can hardly wait." He paused to finish his beer.

"At one point, she informed me that she was half-Jewish and half-Italian. I said, 'That's a splendid combination, Doctor, but under those conditions I have an urgent request: I want your Jewish half to perform the surgery. Okay? All right? Save the Italian part for cooking and singing."

From Gracie's quizzical expression he could tell that his wit was lost on her, the girl being as yet innocent of cultural stereotyping, so he patted her small hand in affectionate appreciation, and, struggling with his crutches, forced himself free of the sofa.

"Here's the deal, pumpkin. Following surgery, I'll be as gimpy as a rusty robot for at least a week, but by the time of your birthday I should be getting around fairly well. You'll be having a party on the big day, I suspect, but the next day, when you've rested from the festivities, we'll go tour the Redhook brewery just as we'd originally planned. Only we won't be freighted there aboard some motorized Prozac box. I'm going to pick up the birthday girl in a stretch limousine. Can you dig it?"

Dig it she could, for she was an excellent digger. And when Moe left, Gracie skipped into the dining room and consumed every drop of the tomato soup, even though by then it was approximately as cold as Moe's Budweiser had been. Then she skipped up the stairs (which is kind of a dangerous practice actually, one you shouldn't attempt without adult supervision), where she changed into jeans and her Give Peace a Chance sweatshirt. She opened her sock drawer and removed a pair of pink ones. She held them at eye level and spoke to them directly. "Socks," she addressed them, "you oughta know the answer to this question: how come Americans tie their shoes too tight?"

Not surprisingly, the socks remained silent, as was their legal right. Gracie, on the other hand, could not suppress a giggle. It would appear that she'd gotten her groove back. But maybe we should keep our fingers crossed for her, wouldn't you agree?

6

The week passed as slowly as a snowman's gas. Each drizzly day limped into the next, as if a falling can of Sapporo had broken the day's sunset toe and torn its sunrise tendon. In kindergarten that week, Gracie was taught nothing she didn't already know; midway through *Finding Nemo*, she suddenly found that thirty-six viewings had been quite enough; and though she badly wanted to visit the recuperating Uncle Moe and bring him a bouquet of flowers or something, her daddy was always too busy to drive her downtown and her mommy was always too tired. It was frustrating.

She did call Moe after his surgery, of course, regretting all the while that she couldn't have made the call on that pink cell phone she was expecting for her birthday and on which niece and uncle might have enjoyed an actual private conversation. And truth be told, it was only the anticipation of her approaching birthday that kept the lights on in her eyes and the skip in her step that week.

Having said all this, however, the week can be described as totally dull and uneventful only if Sunday isn't counted. It's probably permissible to leave out Sunday because in America and Europe, Sunday generally isn't considered a weekday. You yourself must admit that, for various reasons, there's something different about Sundays. Sundays look different, feel different, even smell different than the other six days. Sundays have a different color (usually white), a different texture (starched linen), and a different flavor (kind of like mashed potatoes) than even Saturdays (which are crimson and taste like weenies and beer). In some American cities, incidentally, it's illegal to sell beer on Sundays, but that's a different story.

In any case, an incident occurred that Sunday that wasn't strictly normal, that caused it to further stand out from the week's other days, and that Gracie would not soon forget. It happened in church. (Some silly people used to refer to beer openers as "church keys," but that's a different story, as well.)

For reasons of her own, the Sunday school teacher had directed Gracie to sit in the front row that morning, and being a polite youngster, she obeyed without question or objection, although she was aware that from time to time she might have to hold her nose to keep from gagging.

Taking the third chapter of the Gospel of John as her authority, the teacher had been discoursing forcefully and at considerable length about the necessity to be "born again"—a concept that Gracie, frankly, had never fully comprehended—when she, the teacher, noticed that a shoelace had come undone and bent to tie it (undoubtedly much tighter than function required). Taking advantage of the lull, Gracie impulsively acted to contribute to what so far had been a one-sided discussion.

"My uncle Moe says that when he dies he's gonna be born again as a vinegar eel."

Still in the process of knotting her lace, the teacher commenced to sputter, but before she could straighten up, a curious boy asked, "What's that?"

"Oh," said Gracie in her chirpy voice, "a vinegar eel is a paradise—no, I mean… a para*site*; yeah, that's right, a parasite that lives I think in Germany. It bores into the sides of beer steins over there—they're made outta clay, you know—and it lives on the foam that slops over the top. Uncle Moe…"

"Enough!" screeched the teacher. She seized the startled Gracie by the shoulders and yanked her from her chair. "That'll be enough out of you, little heathen." Her face the color of a grape Popsicle, she pulled Gracie to the door and shoved her through it. "You wait out here until after class. We'll deal with you later."

The Sunday school building was connected to the main church by a colonnade, which, we'd better explain, is a narrow walkway covered by a roof that's supported by columns. One side of this walkway was open to the weather, and you can guess—can't you?—what Seattle's weather was like that morning. (If you said "drizzly," you're a winner.) And because the season was late October, it was also rather chilly. Therefore, when Mrs. Perkel came upon Gracie in the colonnade to which the bewildered girl had been exiled, there was a fair amount of shivering, chattering, and sniffling going on.

As her mother was wrapping a damp and shaky Gracie in her shawl, the teacher arrived on the scene.

"What's she doing out here?" Mrs. Perkel demanded.

Not a bit sorry, the teacher puffed herself up. "Lord knows what sort of loose behavior she's exposed to at home, but I can tell you she was talking in my Sunday school class about *beer* again! And that's not the worst of it." The teacher then repeated, more or less accurately, Gracie's disruptive remarks about dead humans possibly being reborn as German beer worms. "I will not tolerate," railed the teacher, "such depraved pagan garbage being spewed forth in a Christian house of worship!"

For a moment or two, Mrs. Perkel looked the other woman in the eye. Then, slowly, between clenched teeth, she spoke.

"Considering the amount of *wine* consumed by folks in the Bible, including Jesus and his disciples on numerous occasions, holy and otherwise; considering the size of the goblets at the Last Supper, and how our Savior once miraculously transformed ordinary drinking water into the alcoholic beverage of his choice, I doubt that the Good Lord would turn an innocent five-year-old..."

Practically six, Gracie thought, but she kept her mouth shut.

"...out in the cold for merely mentioning a weaker substance like beer. Have you forgotten the part where we were commanded to 'suffer the little children'? As for reincarnation, I personally don't subscribe to it, but tens of millions of decent, intelligent people do, and you'd better pray they're wrong, Miss Righteous. Because if they aren't, you're sure to come back as some hard-shelled pinchy old she-crab with the worst fishy breath in the whole damn ocean." Over her shoulder, she added, "What do you do, eat cat food for breakfast?"

During most of the drive home, neither mother nor daughter spoke. Gracie, however, was beaming with satisfaction, so elated with the unexpected way her mommy had risen to her defense that she could scarcely hold back a giggle.

After a time, Mrs. Perkel herself made a noise that somewhat resembled a laugh, although it could just as easily have been a snort or a loud sigh. She shook her head. "I can't believe it," she said. "I can't believe how much I sounded like Moe back there." She rolled her eyes. "That radical bozo's fancy smart-mouth has been getting on my nerves for seven years, and now I swear I'm starting to sound a lot like like him." She laughed again, although it was hard to tell if she really thought anything was funny.

One block later, she abruptly stopped the car at a strip-mall Häagen-Dazs ice cream parlor, led Gracie inside, and proceeded to buy her a hot fudge sundae as big as the Ritz.

Before Gracie could take her spoon to the treat, however, Mrs. Perkel gripped the child's wrist. "Young lady," she said. Her tone was stern. "There'll be no more nonsense about beer around here. Understood?"

"No more nonsense about beer," Gracie vowed.

She meant what she said, but even as she downsized the sundae, she caught herself wondering what vinegar eels actually look like, and how they would react if one day a reincarnated Uncle Moe showed up in their midst.

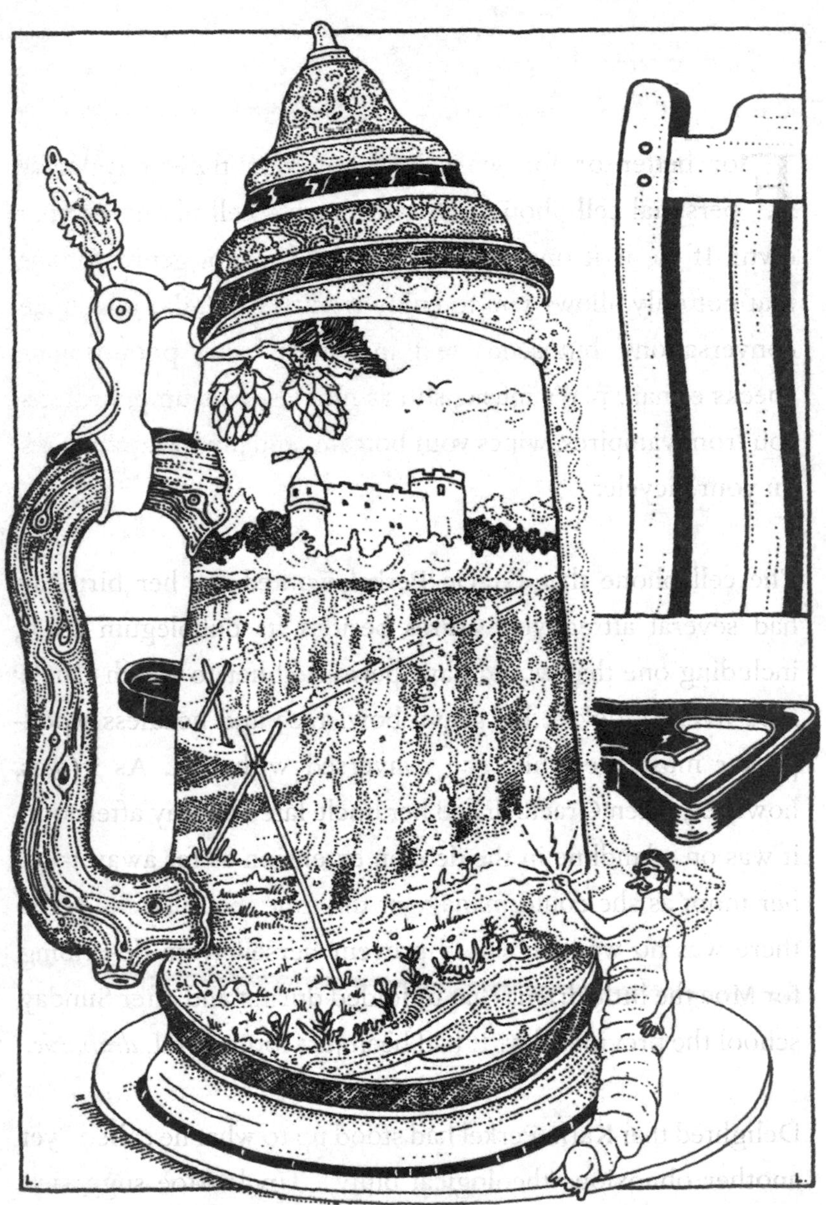

7

For better or for worse, lots of kids these days have personal cell phones. Do you have a cell phone of your own? If so, is it one of those superphones, a genius phone that not only allows you to enjoy traditional audio telephone conversations, but sends text messages, takes photographs, checks e-mail, plays music, shows movies, tells time, protects you from vampires, wipes your bottom, and pumps up the tires on your bicycle?

The cell phone that Gracie Perkel wanted for her birthday had several attractive features besides its bubblegum color, including one that would have permitted her to watch Uncle Moe live, to look at his gravy bowl face and headless woodpecker mustache while she conversed with him. As it was, however, when Gracie dialed her uncle late Monday afternoon it was on a landline in the den, an extension as far away from her mom as she could manage at the time, because she knew there was no way she could prevent herself from describing for Moe the little drama that unfolded during and after Sunday school the previous day. It had been just too... well, *dramatic*.

Delighted that Karla Perkel had stood up to what he called "yet another obnoxious theological bully," Uncle Moe suggested that people such as Gracie's teacher are made smug by their absolute conviction that sooner or later they'll be lounging night and day on a pile of puffy clouds up in Heaven. "Neither I nor anybody else has one pixel of verifiable evidence regarding what happens to us after death, but answer me this, my dear: supposing you die—and I hope you never do—would you, given the choice, rather come back to this life here on Earth as, say, a dolphin, or spend all of eternity as a cloud potato?"

Although concepts such as *eternity* meant little or nothing to Gracie, and even death seemed remote to her—as it must to you, as well—she didn't have to deliberate very long before arriving at a conclusion. "A dolphin would be funner, I think."

"I rest my case. Of course, you did mean to say 'more fun,' instead of 'funner,' but due to your tender age the grammar police won't be writing you a ticket today. After your birthday, though, it could be a different story."

"Uncle Moe, are you really gonna pick me up in a limo-scene?"

"Oops. Sorry, pumpkin, but I see by my crappy flea-market watch that it's already six o'clock. Madeline will be arriving any minute."

“Who’s that?”

“Dr. Madeline Proust.”

“Oh, your po-dock-a-mist.”

“Exactly.”

“She’s coming to your apartment to check on your hurt foot?”

Uncle Moe chuckled. “Yes, I suppose she’ll have a peek at my footsie, but mainly she’s coming to bust a crust.”

“Busta...?”

“You know. Break bread. Share a meal. She dined with me last evening, as well.”

“She must like your cooking.”

He laughed again. “I think she does. I think she does. When we parted last night... umm, well, let me put it this way: Madeline has a way of kissing that could give a bald man a Mohawk.”

Gracie squeaked a soft good-bye, and then just stood there holding the lifeless phone, puzzling once again over the mysterious customs of adults. What was the beautiful pok-a-dye-trist doctor doing kissing on Uncle Moe, who's her patient and kind of unusual looking besides? It wasn't merely their drinking habits that were weird, there seemed to be no end to adult strangeness. Would she be that goofy when she grew up? She remained standing there like that, lost in thought, until, from behind, she heard footsteps enter the darkened den.

"Grace Olivia Perkel!"

Uh-oh. When a parent suddenly hits you with your full birth-certificate handle—first name, middle name, and last—you know that what's coming next is not likely to be pretty. Hasn't that been your experience? It's bad enough when they address you as "young man" or "young lady," but when they serve up the whole enchilada (*William Jefferson Clinton! Oprah Gail Winfrey! Thomas Eugene Robbins!*, or, in this case, *Grace Olivia Perkel!*) the odds are extremely high that you're being strongly warned against the potential commission of some foul deed or other, if, indeed, you haven't already crossed into the naughty zone.

(Have you ever heard an agitated adult or older child exclaim, "Jesus H. Christ!"? It's a vulgar oath, but it may be worth mentioning here that Uncle Moe—full name Morris Norris Babbano, by the way—has offered a ten-dollar reward to anybody who can tell him what the *H* stands for.)

Mrs. Perkel switched on a lamp. In Seattle in October, the day is already so dark by six p.m. that the bats are out shopping for bug bargains and stars are striking wet matches in an attempt to mark a path through the gloom.

"You were talking to Moe, weren't you?"

Gracie hurried to replace the receiver. "Yes, Mommy."

"May I be confident, young lady, that you didn't share any private information with him? Such as my little meltdown after church yesterday?"

So still was Gracie that she could hear her own heart banging. And banging. And banging.

"Because, number one, I'm embarrassed by my outburst, and, number two, the whole mess got started by more of your beer talk, and you've promised me you're keeping your mouth shut about beer from now on. So? Did you tell him or not?"

Oh dear. Gracie didn't want to fib. Fibs were wicked, slippery things. Fibbers start out as spiders and end up as flies. On the other hand, she was equally reluctant to give an honest answer. A truthful response would lead to nothing good. What could she do? Then she remembered something she'd heard from a kid at kindergarten: if you cross your fingers when you're saying words that aren't strictly true, it cancels out the fib; the angels, when they notice your crossed fingers, are tipped off that you don't really mean to be lying, so they sort of wink and let you get away with it.

Encouraged by that information, Gracie slipped her left arm behind her back and crossed her fingers there. "No, Mommy, I didn't say nothing. We were just talking 'bout bald men getting Mohawk haircuts."

Mrs. Perkel rolled her eyes. "Good Lord! That sounds like something that fruitcake would be blabbing about. Give us a break, Moe. Okay, honey, go wash your grubby hands. Your daddy's working late, so you and I are gonna eat our tuna casserole in here where I can watch the news."

Examining her face in the bathroom mirror, Gracie saw a liar staring back at her. Apparently, crossing your fingers doesn't necessarily guarantee protection against a guilty conscience. In her defense, we might console her with the reminder that her fib, while definitely wrong, hadn't really harmed anybody; that it was only a teeny white lie, not one of those huge, black-hearted wholesale lies like the ones important, powerful men are always telling; lies that can cost people money, their reputations, their freedom, or even their lives.

Nevertheless, Gracie was convinced that she was paying the penalty for lying when, four days later, the very day of her birthday, the wings fell off of her dreams, and her bright and bouncy little life seemed to lie scattered in pieces, like a disco ball after an earthquake.

Scorpio
INTENSE
LAGER

8

A disco ball after an earthquake? Let's get serious, kids. Needless to say, that's a ridiculous exaggeration. Yes, but as we've observed, Gracie Perkel did have a bit of a flair for drama, and that's how she might well have described the dismal situation on her birthday—provided, of course, that she knew what a disco ball was. Do you? If not, your parents can tell you. That is, if your parents are cool. Or *were* cool, once upon a time. Back in the day. In the event your grandpa happens to be reading this book to you (everybody's aware that you're quite capable of reading it all by yourself, but let's face it, grandparents are simply mad for reading aloud to their grandkids), there's just no telling what response a question about disco balls might arouse in *him*.

Anyway, the first thing to go wrong was the party. It had to be canceled. It's no secret that every school in the country is a three-ring germ circus, and it seems there was an outbreak of stomach flu at Gracie's kindergarten. The friends she'd invited were either home puking or had been grounded in order to prevent further exposure to the virus.

Then there was the matter of the absent father. Gracie's dad had to go to Tucson on urgent business. Mrs. Perkel rolled those big blue eyes of hers, eyes that her daughter had inherited, and remarked that he was probably playing "urgent golf" with a bunch of Arizona lawyers. Gracie was sure it was a business trip, though, because otherwise why would he have taken his secretary along?

In any case, Mr. P. called to say that he'd ordered Gracie a puppy, but he'd lost the name of the pet store where they were to pick it up. "Next week, for sure," he promised. It was Gracie's turn to roll her eyes. So hard did she roll them that a couple of teardrops fell out and crawled down her cheeks like sow bugs from under a log.

Following vanilla ice cream (she'd requested rocky road) and chocolate cake (why only five candles?), shared with her mommy's girlfriend who lived next door, they spent most of the afternoon driving from mall to mall—the Northgate Mall, the Alderwood Mall, even up north to the Everett Mall—searching for one of those neon-pink cell phones for which Gracie had been pining. Alas, every store was sold out of them, and it was unclear when they would receive a new shipment.

Back home, Mrs. P. served Gracie another slice of cake to comfort her, then went out into the yard to discuss something important, so she said, over the fence with her friend. Gracie was sure that that "something" was her daddy. Had it been a different subject, one they didn't mind Gracie overhearing, they could have discussed it on the telephone. She glanced at the phone then, and noticed that its red light was blinking.

Thinking the recorded message could possibly concern the whereabouts of the misplaced puppy, Gracie punched the voice mail access button. Sure enough, someone began to speak, to speak in a voice that stretched out its words with exaggerated attention, as if it were applying suntan lotion to the bare back of a Hollywood starlet, although sometimes it sounded more like it was milking a snake. True, she hadn't been around much, but so far as she knew there was only one person in the world who talked that way.

"Stand by for a bulletin. A bull has just been seen entering a china shop. How's that for breaking news? Ha ha! Greetings, earthlings. Moe Babbano speaking. I'm out at Sea-Tac Airport, international terminal, passport in hand. Yes, yes indeed, I'm leaving the country again, and this time I don't think I'll be coming back. So to Charlie Perkel, my esteemed, ever-insensitive halfbrother, and to his weary, long-suffering, lovely wife, Karla, I now say, *adios* and thanks for all the opportunities you provided for me to fresco my tonsils with the cardinal brush: that is to say, to drink your beer. Mainly, however, this communiqué is for the birthday girl.

"Gracie, you won't remember this, but when you were an infant, six long years ago, I used to read the encyclopedia to you. It always lulled you to sleep. Especially the volume containing the *Z*'s.

"I don't know if I'm exactly gaga over children, but I do respect them. I respect their deeper feelings and deeper thoughts, layers to which many adults, even the most doting of parents, too often seem oblivious. At any rate, my dear—and this is the point—I've never ever talked down to you, and I have no intention of starting now.

"Here's the deal. Madeline Proust and I have fallen passionately, wildly, crazily in love. A great many birthdays will surely come and go before you'll experience anything remotely resembling this. Indeed, some people never experience it, although they're pretty good at fooling themselves that they do. I can't explain this love, I couldn't explain it to you even if you were twenty-six or thirty-six. The fact that it's totally irrational is part of its appeal.

"This much I can tell you. We're so nuts for each other that Dr. Proust is abandoning her medical practice and I'm skipping out on my apartment—although the postcard collection I'm leaving behind should more than compensate the landlord for any back rent—and in less than an hour we'll be flying off to Costa Rica, where we're intending to permanently reside.

"Costa Rica is downstairs from Mexico. With your mother's help, you can locate it in Volume C of that old encyclopedia that used to provide your bedtime stories. What the map won't tell you is that Costa Rica has done more to preserve its natural environment than any country on Earth, and that it has no army. No navy. No air force. It's hard to believe, isn't it, that any modern government could be that enlightened or any modern population that civilized? Since their government also guarantees free health care, and since it's reasonable to assume that they aren't tying their shoes too tight down there, Madeline's business prospects may be limited, but, hey, it's personal freedom not hundred-dollar bills that lights the soul's cigar, and I hope they're teaching you that in kindergarten.

"There's a lot more to say, Gracie, but we'll be boarding any minute and I've got a pint of Redhook to finish. Obviously, I won't be escorting you to Redhook's brewery tomorrow. Truth is, pumpkin, I'm unsure if I'll ever see you again. Whatever happens, I want you to know..."

Click. Whom-hom-hom-hom. Silence. Apparently, the voicemail recorder had reached its limit. There were no other messages.

Gracie backed away and began to wander around the empty house.

In the kitchen, she was turning in circles, like a dog looking for a soft place to lie down. Her tummy felt like a washer set on Spin Dry. Her heart felt like a balloon from which the air was leaking. Her brain felt like her gums feel after a visit to the dentist.

She was too hurt to stamp her feet or throw things, too angry to weep. She knew she had to do *something*, though, or else she would just curl up in a knot and die.

Eventually, she found herself standing at the refrigerator. Yanking open the door, Gracie suddenly was face to face with a beverage shelf fully stocked with Pepsi cola and beer. She reached in and pulled out a can. She stared at it. She popped its tab. It wasn't Pepsi.

9

Through the lips and over the gums
Look out belly here it comes.

Glug glug glug. The golden liquid was so cold it gave Gracie's teeth a sleigh ride. *Glug glug glug.* It was so bitter it made skunky hair sprout on her tonsils. *Glug glug glug... buurrp!* It was so bubbly it caused her to belch like a Puget Sound ferryboat on a foggy morning. *Glug glug.*

Kids! Listen up! Don't try this at home. It will upset your parents, upset your tummy, and take your brain to places that, guaranteed, will not be as interesting as the places it was eventually to take the brain of Gracie Perkel. For better or for worse, Gracie's experience was a special case. You will see for yourself. But first...

After practically chug-a-lugging the entire can of brew, the six-year-old just stood there in front of the refrigerator, as if guarding its ice cubes from roving gangs of international ice cube thieves. For some reason, her spirits seemed rather rapidly to be improving. In fact, a sense of delicious mischief overtook her, enveloped her to the degree that she suddenly snatched another can of beer out of the refrigerator and, with a whoop, hurled it at her birthday cake, giggling as chocolate frosting splattered from one end to the other of the dining room table.

Borrowing a couple of CDs from her parents' collection (which was strictly against the rules), she carried the discs upstairs to her room, where she shoved one of them, an Aretha Franklin album as it turned out, into her player. Soon she was jumping up and down on the bed (also against the rules), using her hairbrush as a microphone, belting out duets with Aretha.

When the bed began to protest too loudly, to appear on the brink of collapse, she hopped down and commenced to prance, skip, and spin about in what Uncle Moe once called "Gracie's monkey dance of life."

Unfortunately, when the album ended and she paused to rest, she discovered that everything around her was still spinning. The bed, the dresser, and the desk were doing their own monkey dance of life and the walls were lurching and whirling in circles like some kind of theme park ride. The next thing Gracie knew, she was on her hands and knees, throwing up on the Hello Kitty polyester rug: she hadn't even been able to make it to the bathroom.

In a pitifully weak voice, she cried out for her mommy, but Mrs. Perkel was still gabbing in the yard, and anyway, would have been as angry as a chain saw when she discovered the reason for her young daughter's condition. So, using one of her fluffy fuzzy bunny slippers, Gracie wiped clots of chocolaty upchuck from her lips and chin. Then, with a helpless moan, she pulled herself onto the bed.

As you are surely aware, our planet is turning on its axis around and around in space. It turns slowly, however, making one complete rotation only every twenty-four hours; and that's a good thing—isn't it?—because if our world turned as fast as Gracie's room appeared to be turning, the sun would be either rising or setting every fifteen minutes, astronomers would be as woozy as rodeo clowns, and it'd be nearly impossible to keep our meatballs from rolling out of our spaghetti.

Gradually, though, the wallpaper slowed down to regulation Earth speed, and Gracie fell deeply, peacefully asleep. It was a primitive, timeless sleep, free of restless dreams, and she might have slumbered that way for hours had she not been awakened by a gentle but persistent scratching or tapping sensation just below her throat.

When she could focus normally, she saw that a small winged creature of some sort was perched on her upper chest. At first, it looked to be a dragonfly, standing on its hind legs, if dragonflies can be said to have hind legs, but it was pacing to and fro and anybody who's paid attention knows that dragonflies can't walk. Furthermore, it was tapping steadily, purposefully, on Gracie's breastbone with a front leg—or something resembling a leg—as if to get her attention. The thing was only slightly taller than a birthday candle, and had translucent wings that shimmered like moonlight on a barrel of rainwater.

More fascinated than alarmed, Gracie wondered aloud, "What in the world are you?"

Obviously, she wasn't expecting an answer. Obviously. Imagine her intense amazement, therefore, when in a tiny, tinkly but plainly understandable human voice, the creature spoke. "What do you think I am, a Jehovah's Witness? Do I look like I might be selling Girl Scout cookies?" Before a startled Gracie could even attempt a response, it went on to say, "What I am is the Beer Fairy, for crying out loud."

10

Tasting the stale barf in her mouth, Gracie was pretty sure she wasn't dreaming. She rubbed her eyes and stared harder. Sure enough, upon closer inspection, the teeny-weeny creature resembled in almost every detail the fairies whose pictures she'd seen in books. You'd probably agree. In addition to the silvery wings, she (it was definitely female) had flowing red hair, sparkly oversize eyes, a wise, mysterious smile, and a slender, perfectly formed body draped loosely in a strange billowy material that constantly changed color and glittered like diamond dust. She was barefoot, bedecked with a scalloped crown that noticeably resembled a bottle cap, and carried a black leather wand, apparently the instrument with which she had prodded Gracie awake. Gracie was awed, to say the least.

"Are you really the Beer Fairy?"

"Yes, I am."

"I've never heard of a Beer Fairy."

"You have now."

"Hmm. Well, you're very pretty."

"Thank you."

"Where did you come from?"

"Next door."

Gracie's mouth flew open. "You live at the McCormicks'?!" That's where her mommy was. More or less.

The fairy laughed. "Not at your neighbor's house, silly. I mean the world next door to this one."

Gracie nodded. She vaguely understood. "How did you get here?"

"Why, through the Seam."

"The Seam?" Gracie was even more vague about that (just because a person turns six doesn't mean they have to know everything), but she decided to ignore it. "Are you a kind of angel, then?"

"No, no, no. Angels don't do beer. They're into the fine wine and cognac, angels are. They tend to be seriously sophisticated—and if you want my opinion, seriously snootered-up and pucky-wucked. You'll never catch an angel at a kegger, believe me."

"My Sunday school teacher says beer is the Devil's drink."

"Ha! Shows how little she knows about that old boogeyman. For her information, and yours, the Devil drinks Shirley Temples."

"Really!?"

"You can take my word for it."

"Hmm. That's funny. But *you*, Beer Fairy? You're the fairy for beer?"

"Put two and two together, did you? Let me state it this way: if a substantial quantity of beer is being consumed, you can usually expect to find me flitting about the scene."

"Does nobody see you?"

"Yeah, when they drink too much they do, although they don't remember it later. Or if they do remember, they aren't brave enough to admit it." With a soft whir, the fairy flew up then and landed on Gracie's shoulder. "So, what do *you* think of beer, little lady?"

Gracie screwed up her face. "It made me sick."

"That's right. You drank too much too fast and you're way too young."

"When people drink too much beer do you help them?"

"Oh, if they've become pleasantly glad and dizzy, I might take steps to ensure that no real harm befalls them, I might enhance or even participate in their celebration; but should they happen to turn aggressive or nasty or stupid, which isn't uncommon, I'm more likely to kick their butts. Believe me, kiddo, there's not a tough-guy beer guzzler alive whose butt I cannot kick."

"Are you gonna kick my butt?"

Gently shaking her head, the fairy smiled. "No, Gracie Perkel. You've been kicked quite enough today. I'm here to satisfy your unusual curiosity and to reveal to you the origins and mysteries of beer."

"Why?"

"Let's just say that you're a special case. Now, are you ready to take a little trip?"

"A trip? Where? How? My mommy…"

"Don't worry. We're going far away, but we'll be back before you know it. Here. Hang on to my wand."

Ever obedient, Gracie grasped the wand between her thumb and index finger, but it wasn't easy to hold on to, it being not much bigger than a tadpole's tail. Nevertheless, she felt herself being pulled upright from the bed. Whoa! Easy now! With increasing speed, her body was rising toward the ceiling.

"Let's blow this pop stand!" shouted the Beer Fairy—and from the yippee and wahoo exuberance in her voice, anybody could tell it was one of the Beer Fairy's favorite sayings.

Beer

11

For a scary moment, Gracie was sure her skull was about to be smashed like a cantaloupe against the ceiling. She imagined her mother entering the room later and discovering, in addition to the pool of barf, Gracie's splattered brains all over the floor. But then, inches from a head-on collision, there occurred a *poof!* noise, she felt a strong rush of air, and the next thing she knew she was suspended somewhere in the atmosphere. At least, that was her impression.

"What happened?" Gracie asked, in a voice as shaky as a wet chihuahua at a fireworks show.

"We passed through the Seam."

"What Seam?"

"What Seam? The Seam between the Earth and the sky, between the *it* and the *is*, between the fire and the smoke, between the mirror and the reflection, between the buzz and the bee, between the screw and the turning of the screw, and so on and so forth. You get the picture?"

As a matter of fact, in terms of getting the picture, Gracie was between the huh? and the huh-uh. If she neglected to say so, it was because she was too busy straining to see how far she'd fall if she lost her grip on the Beer Fairy's wand. And at that moment, she realized that she was already on the ground, standing amid a waving, seemingly endless expanse of tall, golden-brown grass.

Opening her teeny toothpick arms wide as if to embrace everything in sight, the Beer Fairy announced, "This is where it all begins."

Puzzled, Gracie merely stood there, the grass enveloping her, the seedy spikes at the tip of its stems rubbing against her elbows like the beards of affectionate billy goats. (The grass was up to her armpits, and had she been five instead of six, it might have reached her neck.) The grass was almost crackly dry, yet Gracie could sense the moist heart of the Earth throbbing in it. Was that what the Beer Fairy meant about it all starting here?

"This is a grain field," the sprite explained. "A field of barley, to be specific. All beer gets its start as grain. Some pretty tasty beer is made from wheat; Asians brew an acceptable beer from rice, though it's not my cup of tea, and there're Africans who resort to millet for a brew that's dipped warm out of buckets on village market day—neither better tasting nor less filling, I'm afraid—but the worldwide grain of choice for making beer is good old barley." She performed a loop and landed on a stalk top, which bowed ever so slightly from her cottony weight.

"My uncle Moe says beer's made outta hops."

"Your uncle Moe is full of you-know-what. Or else you misunderstood him." The Beer Fairy thrust her wand toward Gracie. "Come along. With that in mind, we'd better get to our next stop."

"Are we blowing this pop stand?" asked Gracie.

The Beer Fairy laughed a fairy laugh. "You're okay, kiddo. You're all right. Now, treat yourself to a good long look at this barley field as we lift off. You can appreciate its rustic beauty, I'm sure, but you could never guess what history or what forces lie hidden in that common crop.

"Barley grains found near Al Fayyūm, Egypt, have been shown in laboratory tests to be 5,000 years old. That's 4,994 years older than you, little miss. Whether barley—originally just another species of wild grass—was actually domesticated in Egypt way back then, or was imported as livestock feed from more agriculturally advanced northern cultures, is a subject scholars can debate until their glasses fog over. A more interesting subject is how the Egyptians figured out a way to convert that donkey chow, that camel fodder, into an intoxicating beverage in the first place, an inebriating liquid refreshment so wholly perfect that it's endured and spread and has grown ever more popular through the ages.

"For whatever reason, the ancient Egyptians weren't satisfied with mere survival. They wanted to be remembered forever, which is why they built the pyramids, and they wanted to ensure that they'd be sufficiently glad and dizzy during their lifetime, which is why they invented beer."

"Did the Egypt people invent you, too?"

"Ha! You *are* the inquisitive one, aren't you? No, they invented me only in the sense that your mommy and daddy's love invented you. But that's another story. Right now, we need to go."

That suited Gracie fine. The mention of her parents made her think of home, and that talk about ancient Egyptians had made her miss Uncle Moe. Such thoughts were threatening to spoil her big birthday adventure. She need not have worried, though, because as they rose above the farmland, there was another *poof!*, another whoosh of wind, and in a wink she and the Beer Fairy were out of the sunlight, out of the sweet country air; were, in fact, indoors somewhere, inside a room that was chilly, smelly, and darn near as vast as a barley field.

12

"Can you guess where we are?" asked the Beer Fairy.

Gracie glanced around the building, letting her eyes adjust to the artificial light. The place just looked like some dumb factory to her. Finally, for the heck of it, she sang out, "Costa Rica!"—knowing perfectly well it wasn't true.

"Notice that huge pile of sacks on that wooden platform over there. What do you think is in those sacks?"

"Uh, flour."

"No."

"Sugar."

"Not exactly."

"Cement."

"Guess again."

"Kittens."

"*Kittens?* What's the matter with you, girl? Think. Where were we just now?"

"Egypt."

"Oh, for goodness sake! Listen, I'm the Beer Fairy, I can tolerate a lot of goofiness—if it wasn't for goofy business I'd practically do no business at all—but you've gone and gotten your six-year-old self involved with beer and I'm making a sincere effort to teach you something about the substance you're dealing with. Now, I promised not to kick your butt, but if you…"

"Oh, I remember now!" Gracie flashed her brightest smile. "We were on a farm for barley."

"Hey, hey! A barley field. Congratulations." If you never thought fairies could be sarcastic, think again. "Didn't that uncle of yours ever tell you that nobody likes a smart-ass?"

Gracie tried half-heartedly to recall such sage advice, but all that came to mind was Moe's warning that "Every time a person goes to the mall, she loses a little piece of her soul."

The truth of the matter is that Gracie had been far more

interested in the wee winged creature hovering a few inches in front of her nose than she'd been in these new surroundings, whether indoors or out, and she'd experienced difficulty concentrating on the brewski lessons. You'd have much the same reaction, don't you think? At any rate, Gracie resolved to both watch her mouth and pay closer attention, and she was all ears as the Beer Fairy continued.

"Okay then, it's barley grains—which is to say, barley *seeds*—that are in those sacks. However, between the time the grain was harvested in the field and the time it was funneled into the sacks, it was messed with, it was altered. The barley's been *malted*."

Visions of Häagen-Dazs milkshakes jumped instantly into Gracie's brain. She shooed them away. She was doing her best to be an attentive pupil.

"The grains were soaked in water for approximately two days to speed them along toward sprouting, the first step in a seed's development into a plant. During this germination period, as it's called, the natural starch in the barley breaks down into a simple kind of sugar whose purpose, according to the plan of nature, is to nourish the baby plant."

Baby plants being nourished by sugar! A delighted Gracie thought that was too cute for words. She almost squealed.

"Ah, but before this process gets very far," the Beer Fairy went on, "before the grain actually sprouts, it's heated in a kiln to bring the germination to a screeching halt, right when the newly formed sugar is reaching its peak. At this point, it's become what we call *malted barley*, and the sacks of it are ready to be emptied into a masher. What happens there, do you suppose?"

"Something gets mashed."

"Brilliant deduction. The malted grain is crushed into a fine powder, which in turn is emptied into one of those tall stainless steel water tanks over there. The water—with the mash in it, of course—is then heated to 156 degrees."

"That sounds pretty hot."

"Just a balmy day on the beach for a Sugar Elf, but for humans and most other life-forms…"

Gracie interrupted. "There's Sugar Elfs?!"

"Forget about them. It's enough to know that if there was no such thing as sugar, there'd be no such thing as beer. As the mashed grain cooks in the hot water, in fact, its remaining starch is converted by heat and moisture into other sugars that are more complex, more advanced, than the malted ones."

Noticing that Gracie looked confused, the Beer Fairy suggested that she consider malt as kindergarten or first-grade sugar, while the mash-tank sugar was high school or maybe community college sugar.

Gracie wasn't buying the sugar bit. "But beer is *bitter*," she objected.

"That's where your uncle's hops come in. While the mash is being cooked, before it's strained out of the sugar-heavy water and disposed of, hop petals or else pellets made from compressed hop flowers (the pellets look exactly like pet-store hamster food, by the way) are dumped into the tanks. Hops reduce the sweetness of the mixture and add flavor and aroma. Without hops, Redhook and Budweiser would be little more than cloudy sugar water.

"Okay, then, we've added our hops, but, Gracie, we still don't have beer. Instead we have a tank of flavored liquid the brewers refer to as *wort*."

"Ooo." Gracie made a face. "My cousin had a wart on his behind."

"That's something altogether different."

"Well, it's still kind of an ugly word."

"I guess I'd have to agree. *Malt* and *mash* and *hops* and *yeast* aren't exactly puffs of pure poetry, either. For that matter, the English word *beer* itself (evolved from the older word *beor*) is not the most musical little tittle of elegant language ever to roll off a tongue. However, as Shakespeare once said..."

"Who's that?"

"A famous guy who wrote a lot about fairies. You'll read him someday. Knowing you, you'll probably act—and try to steal a scene or two—in one of his plays. Shakespeare said that a rose by any other name would smell as sweet."

"What's that mean?"

"It means that if beer had been called *champagne*, *holy water*, or *potassium cyanide*, it would be no more—or no less—wonderful. It also means that if your name was Gertrude or Hortense or Annabella, you'd be just as pretty, just as sensitive, just as lively and curious—and just as much a pain in the butt—as you are when your name is Gracie. Now for goodness sake, child, let's get on with it!"

13

It's rather obvious that Gracie and the Beer Fairy were touring a brewery. Right? In this brewery, as in every brewery, there would have been men working: busy brewers all over the place. Right? Yet the men had failed to take the slightest notice of the presence in their midst of a strange little girl in a vomit-stained birthday dress with a ginger-haired, gossamer-gowned "dragonfly" on her shoulder. Right? But being smart, you've guessed (correctly) that Gracie and the fairy couldn't be observed, were invisible to the men due to the fact that they were on the Other Side of the Seam. Right?

Or, if you didn't figure that out on your own, your grandpa surely pointed it out to you—provided he's still hanging in there with you, which he may well be since your grandpa, after so many, many experiences of reading you bedtime stories about talking choo-choo trains, teddy bear picnics, and the hardships of young Abe Lincoln, stories that surely made his teeth feel squeaky and his eyelids droop like coffin covers, well, he must have jumped at the chance to read you a book about *beer*; must have been so enthused that he poured himself a tall frosty one before he began—and if Grandma hasn't been checking on him, perhaps a couple more by Chapter 13. Right? It wouldn't be unusual. That's often the way it is with beer.

That's the way it is with beer, but so far we've encountered no actual beer in this brewery. Rather, the tour has stalled before some huge tanks of warm water, flavored (heavily at some breweries, lightly at this one) with malt and hops. (It may be worth mentioning here that the water used in brewing also contributes to the character of beer: for example, hard water—water with a lot of mineral content, such as that in Ireland—lends a muscular nature to a stout brew like Guinness, while softer, less mineral-laced water such as that for which the Czech Republic is famous, produces the paler, crisper style of beer known worldwide as *pilsner* or *lager*.)

At any rate, at this point the Beer Fairy, growing a tad impatient, hustled Gracie along to a second, equally large set of tanks: the fermentation vessels. "This is where the rabbit jumps out of the hat. This is where the so-so hits the go-go and lets loose the mojo. This is where beer becomes beer."

The transformative agent, the freelance sorcerer whose alchemy turns wort into beer, is *yeast*. Once the wort has cooled and has been transferred into fermentation tanks, yeast is summoned to the tanks and left undisturbed therein for at least ten days to do the mysterious work that yeast and yeast alone can do.

Although she was aware that her mother used something called yeast when she baked bread, Gracie had not the remotest idea what the stuff was (for a time she believed yeast to be the opposite direction from west), so the Beer Fairy had to explain.

"Yeast is a miniature plant, a fungus actually, a cousin of mushrooms and toadstools; but while each mushroom is composed of numerous cells, a yeast plant is so tiny it's got only one cell to its name. To see a yeast plant, you'd need a microscope, although you'd have no problem locating yeast plants to look at, because they're floating around in the air almost everywhere; not just in breweries or in the woods and fields, but in your house, the White House, the Vatican, and a rock star's dressing room. Maybe especially in a rock star's dressing room."

In spite of being assured that yeast plants were microscopic in size, Gracie couldn't keep herself from staring hard at the air around her. Just in case. She didn't want to miss anything.

"You may be wondering how all that yeast got into the planet's atmosphere in the first place." In the event Gracie was wondering that very thing, the fairy went on to suggest that over countless eons of time, yeast spores may have accidentally—or on purpose—drifted down through empty space like friendly invaders from other planets far, far away. "It's scientifically feasible. They definitely possess the physical capability to do just that. Beer, then, has not only a deep connection to the soil beneath us but also to the stars." After a brief pause to allow the girl to muse on beer's possible links to Mars, to Venus, to space travel and little green men, the sprite brought her back down to earth.

"There are people who earn a living cultivating yeast plants and molding them by the tens of millions into cakes or powders. This is the yeast that brewers dump in the wort. There's nothing yeast likes to eat better than wort. To hungry yeast, wort is like a steak dinner with chocolate mousse for dessert. Well, actually, for yeast, wort is more on the order of pecan pie à la mode with chocolate mousse for dessert, because what the yeast feasts on in the wort is the sugar. And as it digests it, yeast slowly turns that sugar into *alcohol*. Bingo!"

"Alcohol makes beer beer, and people want beer because they want alcohol."

"Oh, beer does possess other charms, Gracie; but in the end, you're correct: that's what it comes down to. Yeast, like malt and hops and water, influences the character and flavor of beer, but its primary business, its day job, the work that pays its rent and makes it famous—in a funky sort of way—is to give sugar an extreme makeover. The people in the lab coats call that makeover process *fermentation*. What the Sugar Elves call it is something else again."

"There's Sugar Elfs?"

"Never mind them. Sugar is reliable, dependable; you can count on sugar to teach cakes and cookies to sing their sweet little songs, to grin from ear to ear whenever it lands on your tongue, and, when you aren't looking, to rot your molars and make you fat. It's all very predictable. But by the time yeast gets through fermenting it, sugar will gradually have turned into something wild and crazy; into that tricky, loose-cannon, charismatic chemical known as alcohol.

"It was the alcohol in beer that set you to merrily dancing, and it was the alcohol that made you puke. Alcohol. It has that power, and we can discuss its good side and its bad side to our hearts' content. But listen: thirty-six billion gallons of beer are sold in the world every year. How much beer do you suppose would be sold if there wasn't any alcohol in it?"

The little girl pondered this, but not for long. "About a gallon and a half," she suggested.

14

Uncle Moe had told Gracie that once in a strange, distant land (it could have been England, she wasn't certain) he'd visited a village called Creamed-Beef-on-Toast. She'd giggled, thinking he was probably being silly. Now, however, as from the hilltop on which she and the Beer Fairy had come to rest, Gracie looked down on a village in the valley below; she had a funny feeling that that village was the very place to which Moe had referred. She couldn't explain it, so she kept quiet, lest the Beer Fairy think *she* was the silly one, which the fairy surely would had she blurted out, "Look down there! That's Creamed-Beef-on-Toast."

Prior to departing the brewery, the pixie had guided Gracie down a spiral metal staircase to another large room filled with yet more large tanks. "These are the conditioning tanks," the fairy had said. "After the primary fermentation is done, the immature beer travels through pipes down to here, where it's allowed to age, usually for about two weeks. As part of its conditioning it's generally filtered to strain out any remaining yeast. Some brewers will leave particular beers unfiltered, however, so they can continue to age in the bottle. Children such as you, Gracie, are best left unfiltered while you age, although some parents and institutions, regrettably, do attempt to filter the young souls in their charge."

"Uncle Moe told me no institution can be trusted," said Gracie, not that she completely understood what he'd meant by "institution". The Beer Fairy nodded but didn't respond. Maybe she was tired of hearing about that guy Moe.

"The process here is almost over," she said instead. (Gracie wasn't too unhappy about that, because the temperature in the conditioning room was only thirty-four degrees.) "You see that giant horizontal tank over there next to the doors? That's a holding tank. When the beer at last has satisfied all the brewmaster's expectations, it's passed into the holding tank, ready now to leave the brewery in kegs or bottles or, if it's a macrobrewery, in cans, as well. It will journey out into the world as though flying a flag, bearing the brand name of the brewing company."

"You mean like Re-Re-Redhook?" asked Gracie. Her teeth were starting to chatter.

"Could be Redhook. Or Red Stripe, or Red Tail, or Red MacGregor, Red Horse, Redback, Red Erik, or Red Dog. It could be Black Dog, Laughing Dog, Sun Dog, Turbodog,

Dogfish Head, Hair of the Dog...."

"I kno-know about that!"

"...Black Eye, Black Gold, Black Mac, Black Butte, Blue Label, Blue Moon, Blue Heron, or Pabst Blue Ribbon. It could be, as long as we're doing colors, Great White. It could be Lazy Boy, Beach Bum, Dead Guy, Fat Tire, Rolling Rock, Three Philosophers, or Delirium Nocturnum.

"In Japan, it could be Kirin, Asahi Super Dry, Yebisu, or Sapporo."

Gracie knew about Sapporo, as well, but she didn't say anything.

"In Germany, there're so many it's impossible to know where to begin. And Belgium has 365 brands, one for every day of the year. The Czech Republic..."

"What about Co-Co-Costa Rica?"

"The national beer of Costa Rica is Imperial, although I don't know why you're so interested in that toy country. Anyway, enough brand naming. It could go on all day." She'd led Gracie out onto the loading dock, where delivery trucks would eventually come to pick up the kegs or the cases of bottles. On the dock there'd been a splash of sunlight, like a puddle of spilled lager, and Gracie went and stood in it. Her jaws quit banging their drumsticks.

Hovering like a miniature helicopter, a rescue chopper for wounded ladybugs, the fairy, with a serious face, announced that the time had arrived "to learn the truth of beer."

Gracie, who'd recently been paying studious attention to all the tanks and tubes and materials, was surprised and confused. "But I already learned..."

"No, no. You've learned something about the chemistry of beer, the technology of brewing, that's correct, but a brewery doesn't define beer any more than a shoe factory defines dancing."

"I dance in my sneakers," Gracie volunteered.

"Good. But it's not about the sneakers, is it?"

"No, 'cause sometimes I dance barefooted."

"Would you say you dance because you're glad and dizzy?"

"I don't know. I guess so. Uncle Moe says that when I dance I look like a blissed-out monkey."

"You're not alone, kiddo, you're not alone. When civilized people dance they reconnect with their old animal nature. It reminds them that they aren't mechanical chess pieces or rooted trees, but free-flowing meat waves of possibility."

Gracie looked as blank as a crashed computer, an empty wading pool, a stuffed owl; leading the fairy to say, "Well, enough about dancing. Our subject is beer. If beer is more than the sum of its parts, if the truth of beer lies beyond the brewery, where do we go to find it, and why should we care?"

Immediately upon posing the question, the Beer Fairy had thrust her wand at Gracie, who automatically took hold of it. Within minutes, or maybe even seconds (*poof! whoosh!*), the brewery was out of sight and the pair of them were seated on a grassy hilltop, overlooking, on one side, fields of ripe grain that stretched into the distance like gulfs of whiskered honey; and on the other, a village that may or may not have been Creamed-Beef-on-Toast.

15

It was nice to be outdoors again. The day remained quite sunny, although shuffling along the horizon was a big bumpy cloud the color of the bruises that decorated Gracie's shins whenever she played soccer.

When you look at the sky, do the shapes of particular clouds remind you of animals or furniture or various objects? You're not alone. Gracie, for example, thought this blue-black cloud resembled a bag lady, it being ragged and droopy and slow and dirty looking, with occasional darker bulges of suspended rainwater that could be viewed perhaps as Dumpster diamonds or wads of bag-lady underwear. She imagined the sun giving the poor cloud a handout to buy itself a cup of coffee—or just go away.

Briefly, Gracie wondered if this cloud might actually be lumbering above Seattle, way off in the distance, and she felt a pang in her heart. It was a twinge, however, that could not accurately be described as "homesickness," at least not in the usual sense.

Turning her back on the cloud, Gracie directed her gaze to that village that clung to the banks of a river in the valley down below. Some sort of festival was in progress there, and the cobblestone streets were teeming with noisy merrymakers. There were carnival games and dancing. There were flags fluttering, sausages smoking on grills. The music that drifted up the hillside was polka music, a style with which Gracie was unfamiliar and which struck her as more than a little goofy.

She saw a great many people seated at tables in tavern gardens, while waiters in long white aprons rushed from bars to tables, back and forth, bearing whole trays of mugs that overflowed with foam. Obviously, large quantities of beer were being both consumed and spilled. Vinegar eels would be having a field day.

The Beer Fairy, too, was observing this activity, and eventually, as if she felt she ought to get on with her teaching, she said, "Beer is rooted in the Four Elements. Do you know the Four Elements? They are Earth, Air, Fire, and Water. Together they form the basis of what some like to call the real world.

"Barley and wheat spring from the Earth, of course. The grain is heated to make malt and the malted mash is cooked: that's where Fire comes in. As for Water, that's a no-brainer, since beer is essentially enhanced Water."

The sprite paused, prompting Gracie to ask, "What about the Air elephant?" It was amazing how attentive she'd become.

"Why, the Air is in the bubbles. In the carbonation. You'll learn at school that the Air you inhale is oxygen and the Air you breathe out is carbon dioxide. It's carbon dioxide bubbles—carbonated Air—that causes beer to sparkle, to tease the inside of one's cheeks with delicious prickles, and, yes, to make one belch. A degree of carbonation occurs naturally while beer is fermenting, but some brewers will later add carbon dioxide to the conditioning tanks to produce a more bubbly brew."

Gee, I thought we were done with the brewery lessons, thought Gracie. She struggled in vain to hold back a yawn.

"Something you'll never learn in school *or* in a brewery," the Beer Fairy went on, poking Gracie between the eyes with her wand, "is that there's also a Fifth Element. That's right, another basic component of reality, one that's as nourishing as Earth, as shifty as Water, as invisible as Air, and as dangerous as Fire."

There's nothing like the word *dangerous* to generate interest: it's irresistible to young males, scary to most young females, though not necessarily those of the Gracie Perkel variety.

"What is it?" she asked.

The fairy hesitated. A breeze rustled her papery wings. "It's not easy to say." She paused again. "I'm only labeling it an 'element,' understand, because it doesn't fall into the category of animal or vegetable or mineral. It disobeys the laws of physics and it moons the rules of logic, just as the two of us have been doing today, actually, although you seem to have taken it completely in stride. What is it? Some people call it *transcendence*, some used to call it *magic*... before that word got used up.

"It's a mixture of pure love, unlimited freedom, and total, spontaneous, instantaneous knowledge of everything past, present, and future—all rolled up in a kind of invisible ghost-sheet enchilada that can be periodically smelled and occasionally tasted, but rarely chewed and never, never digested. Hey, you don't need to make a face. I told you it wouldn't be easy.

"There are those who regard it as a blast of divine energy, originating in Heaven, maybe, or in Another World. There're also people who are content to refer to it simply as the *Mystery*, and that's as good a term as any, I guess, although I'm rather fond of the jazz musician who, in a different context, once called it *hi de ho*."

Gracie issued half a giggle. The top half. She wasn't sure why. "Hi de ho," she said. And then she said it again.

"People are attracted to the Mystery," said the fairy, only to immediately correct herself. "No, not simply attracted, they are unconsciously pulled toward it, they hunger for it, they yearn to connect with it, to get next to it, even to merge with it."

"They do?"

"They do and always have, although as I said, this longing is deep inside and mostly unconscious."

"But what is it?"

"If we could say what it is, it wouldn't be the Mystery, would it? When you stare out of your window into the drizzle and the mist, don't you sometimes feel that there's something more to life than what television and the mall and kindergarten and even your family represent; that there's something grander and stranger, more alive, more free and more real than what any ordinary situation has to offer? Something way *beyond*? And that it seems to be calling to you, calling even though it doesn't know your name, your address, how old you are, or give a rip if you've washed behind your ears or finished your peas?"

"I guess so."

"The older you get—and this is a good thing to remember on your birthday, Gracie—the harder it is to interface with the Mystery. Yet adults still thirst for that connection, that alternative to the unsatisfying reality men have constructed for themselves, and which they feel locked into like a dungeon.

"So, they resort to all sorts of things—a few enlightened, many destructive, most ineffective, some just plain silly—that might allow them even a breath or two outside the prison walls. To a certain extent, that explains the appeal of beer."

"It unlocks them?"

"Well, it temporarily loosens their ties to the stressful world of work and responsibility."

"Like loosening shoelaces that are tied too tight?"

"Exactly. That's pretty smart, kiddo. How do you come up with these things?"

Gracie blushed. "Hi de ho," she said.

Tired of sitting, perhaps, the Beer Fairy suddenly rocketed up in the air, where she performed an acrobatic triple loop a few inches from Gracie's nose. By no means, however, was she done talking. "Let me be clear," she said as she hovered, "beer is not a part of the actual Mystery or even connected to it in any direct way. No, no. Beer is merely a vehicle.

"On rare occasions, and for very brief moments, that vehicle may carry a person beyond the state of being glad and dizzy (and I'm all for glad and dizzy, you know, glad and dizzy is my neighborhood); may shoot them through an opening *between* the glad and the dizzy..."

"Is it like Alice's rabbit hole to Wonderland?"

"It's much smaller than that."

"Like a mouse hole?"

"Smaller. More like a crack in the egg of a barley beetle."

"Oh."

"Beer, if it's just the right amount—not too little and definitely not too much—may on occasion transport one through that crack and carry one close enough to the gates of the Mystery so that one's granted a quick but entirely rapturous peek inside."

"What's it look like?"

The fairy smiled and rotated her wings. "Everything. And nothing. Both at the same time. What does the electricity inside your atoms look like? What do forever and laughter and liberty look like? It's the face everybody shared before they were born and the joke they'll finally get after they're dead. It's the meaning of meaning, the other that has no further, and the which of which there is no whicher."

While Gracie was trying vainly to picture such a thing, her wee guide said, "Be warned. When considering beer as a vehicle, one had better bear in mind that it's hardly reliable transportation. It's a very old cart, in fact; a wagon pushed and pulled by forgotten forces, by agricultural spirits, the ancient spirits of grain and the land. It's a wagon, my dear, that can easily swerve and run off the road."

Now, kids, if that grandpa of yours hasn't given up and wandered off to watch a ball game on TV, he may well be skipping over this part of the story, believing that you couldn't possibly relate to all this stuff about a Fifth Element, about the Mystery, about magic, ancient grain spirits, and so forth.

He's wrong, isn't he? Because almost every child between the ages of, say, three and twelve (and a few lucky ones much older) seems at least vaguely aware of the presence of a separate reality: some half-familiar, magical Other World that, even when spooky or threatening, both thrills and nurtures them more than the reality that modern adult society would have them buy into. Do you agree? And do you think now might be the time to encourage gramps to pop open another brewski?

In any event, before the fairy could say more (if, indeed, she intended to say more), she and Gracie were startled by the sound of screaming and crying. They turned to see a terrified young woman clawing her way up the grassy hillside, while close behind, two men pursued her, smirking, panting, and lurching, obviously intending to do her harm.

16

As the shrieking maiden, wild-eyed and bloody-kneed, neared the summit of the hill, the Beer Fairy was the first to act. Like a redheaded bullet with its pants on fire, she sent herself zinging at the nearest of the two pursuers. She circled his head, poking him in the eye, then the ear, then the eye again, with her wand. Around and around his head she buzzed, her wings whirring, her wand stabbing.

The fellow must have believed he'd disturbed a nest of oversize, particularly disagreeable bees. Cursing the entire insect species and the Satan who surely created it, he swatted furiously at the fairy, who continued to circle his head with blurry speed. She rammed her wand up his nostril. He snorted. She shoved it in his ear. He yelped. Turning in circles, he was fast becoming dizzy, though anything but glad. The fact that he was intoxicated to begin with didn't help his coordination.

Finally, however, one of his swats connected. He was a hefty farmboy type and the strength of his swat sent the dainty pixie hurtling head over heels to the turf. Stunned, she lay in the grass, breathing hard, crown askew, her tiny back throbbing with pain.

Meanwhile, the young woman had reached the hilltop, where she stumbled forward, allowing the second attacker to catch up with her. Before she could regain her feet, he grabbed her roughly by the wrist. Although out of breath, he was sniggering, and cooing some insane kind of baby talk.

Gracie knew she must intervene—but how? For one thing, she couldn't remember which side of the Seam she was on. She thought that after they'd poofed out of the brewery, she and the fairy had returned to This Side, but she couldn't be sure; and if they had not, neither the attacker nor his victim could see or hear her.

Uncertain just how to proceed, she ran up to the big snockered lout and yelled in her deepest voice (which was not much deeper than the chirp of a nervous cricket), "Stop! Let her go, you stupid man!" The lout didn't release the hysterical woman, but his leer switched to an expression of great surprise. What was this child doing here? Apparently, he'd heard and seen Gracie all too well, and was now looking around frantically to ascertain whether or not she was accompanied by adults.

Back in early September, when Mr. Perkel had been the coach of Gracie's peewee soccer team—this was before a group of the soccer moms had banded together and fired him—he'd drilled his daughter over and over on what he called the "lawyer kick." It was a way to kick an opposing player in the leg so hard she'd topple over and have to leave the game, yet was so sneaky that most of the time the referee would fail to notice it, so wouldn't assess a penalty. Gracie considered it a dirty trick and she never tried it, but she remembered it perfectly well.

The lawyer kick was delivered to the man's shin with the full force of six-year-old indignation. "Hai dozo!" Gracie yelled as she kicked, imitating a cry she thought she remembered from martial arts movies. "Go go Tokyo!" she yelled, and kicked again. Already unsteady from excessive drink, the attacker lost his balance and dropped to one knee, maintaining, nonetheless, his grip on the woman. It was then that Gracie shouted, "Sapporo! Chop suey!" and kicked again. This time the kick accidentally landed higher. Much higher.

For a couple of seconds, the drunken brute seemed to be sucking in all the oxygen from the surrounding countryside. He gasped. Then he groaned. Then he rolled over onto his side. Because he was at the very edge of the hilltop, he, against his will, continued to roll. His body went tumbling more than a third of the way down the hill before its progress was stopped by a juniper bush. He lay there, in no apparent rush to get up.

While this was occurring, the fairy was rubbing her aching spine, flexing her rumpled wings, struggling to get back on her own two fect. She was done with her horror-movie bee imitation. Henceforth, she'd leave buzz-bombing to the hornets. From a sitting position, she pointed her wand at the lummox who'd swatted her. As if undecided in which direction to move, he was shifting his bleary gaze from the sobbing maiden a few yards above him to his friend who lay unmoving farther down the slope. The fairy took aim. She fired a single amber beer ray at the area behind his eyes where his brain ought to be.

It was a ray she'd used countless times before to subdue quarrelsome sailors, rampaging soccer goons, and obnoxious fraternity boys, and she should have used it sooner on this occasion, but she'd been so angry and upset she'd lost her cool. When it struck its target, the beer ray would instantly raise the alcohol level in an imbiber's blood to such a degree that his lights would begin to flicker, his curtains commence to close, and his internal clock to chime midnight. Now this farmhand, when hit, staggered back a few steps before stumbling blindly back down the hill, collapsing, and passing out cold beside his pal.

The fairy flew, if one could call such a wobbly display flying (she resembled some variety of popcorn moth trapped in an automatic popper), to Gracie's side, landing with uncharacteristic clumsiness on the child's shoulder. Together, silently, the two watched the young woman make her way down the opposite side of the hill, moving as fast as she dared without losing her footing. She appeared to be heading toward a distant farmhouse nestled between two barley fields.

"That must be her family's farm," said the fairy at last. "She looks a mess. Her folks will think she's had too much beer at the festival and order her to bed without any strudel."

Gracie was fixing to comment on how unfair that would be when the Beer Fairy suddenly kissed her. (You'll probably never in your life be kissed by a fairy, but should you be, you'll know it, and you'll treasure that kiss forever.) "You were very brave, kiddo," the fairy said. "Very brave, indeed."

"Thanks," said Gracie. "Hi de ho."

"I want to show you something, braveheart. Down there in the town."

"You mean in Creamed-Beef-on-Toast." Since she was so brave, Gracie thought she might as well say it. She'd show her tiny guide she was not only courageous but also knew her geography.

The fairy looked puzzled. "What the heck are you talking about, child?"

"The name of the town: Creamed-Beef-on-Toast."

"Are you joking? Whoever heard of such a place? The name of that town happens to be Pimple-on-Chin."

"Yuck!" said Gracie.

Considering that in seven years or so, Gracie would doubtlessly sprout pimples of her own—as will you, provided you aren't pimpled already—it was scarcely an appropriate response.

17

"Suppose, for example," said the fairy, who was increasingly showing signs of recovery from the blow she'd suffered, "that an airliner is flying over Pimple-on-Chin, bound for, say, Seattle."

Automatically, Gracie looked to the sky. She saw acres of blue, a gradually lowering sun, and a skinny white elbow of moon, but no plane. It was only an example.

"And suppose," the sprite continued, "that aboard that aircraft there's a passenger who's on her way to Seattle to murder her brother so as to claim his share of an inheritance. Also aboard that same flight, there's a second woman, a physician, a noted specialist, who's traveling to Seattle to perform a surgery that will save an infant's life.

"The airplane itself is neither good nor evil, is it? It's a vehicle, a neutral, unattached object, kind of like a knife that can be used for peeling turnips in an orphanage or for slicing off a man's ears. Many things in life are like that, including, and perhaps most especially, people's political and religious beliefs—but that's a subject for a much later day. What you need to remember now is that matters are very seldom all black or all white. They can even be both at the same time."

The fairy looked to see if Gracie was taking any of this in. She pointed again at the village of Pimple-on-Chin.

"You've just witnessed how beer can contribute to vile behavior. If one is rude, beer can make one ruder; if one is a slob, it can make one sloppier; if one is mean, it can make one meaner; if one's dumber than one looks… well, you get the picture. Beer can lead weak men to think they're mighty, and foul-mouthed women to believe themselves amusing and hip. Worse, if one is cursed with an addictive personality, it can bring on the serious disease of alcoholism.

"On the other hand, you've learned that every day, beer helps millions to be glad and dizzy, and that once in a great while it can lead to a brush with the Mystery." She paused, as if to reflect. "As long as there are those who seek contact with the Mystery, no matter how misguidedly and crudely they go about it, I suppose there's still hope for the human race."

Pausing again, as if to permit her words to sink in, the pixie gestured toward one end of the village. "There's something else. You see that beer garden that's closest to the water? Yes? Can you make out that soldier in uniform who's sitting alone at the bar, staring at the river? At sunset, he's expected to rejoin his regiment, and they'll march off in the night to fight a bloody battle in some stupid war that in the end will benefit nobody but the rich and powerful, and maybe not even them. The soldier has been contemplating making a run for it, but fear has held him back.

"Okay, now do you see that other fellow who's just rather awkwardly, hesitantly approached a table of young women and asked one of them to dance?"

Gracie did see him, though she was still stealing glances at the sky, looking for that airplane.

"That guy is desperately in love. He wishes to ask the girl to marry him, but so far he's been too timid to pop the question."

While they stood spying on the scene at the beer garden, the soldier nonchalantly slipped off of the bar stool and very slowly made his way, in a zigzag route, to the river's edge. When, glancing repeatedly over his shoulder, he was confident none in the noisy crowd was looking his way, he stepped out of his boots and slid into the water, slid so smoothly he made scarcely a ripple. He swam, unobserved, to the other shore, which was heavily wooded.

Meanwhile, the shy man had drawn his beloved off of the dance floor to a relatively quiet corner beside some rose bushes. He was down on one knee before her.

"You see," said the fairy, "the beer has dissolved enough of their fear to allow the men to act. Now, many would call this 'false courage,' and they might be right. But there are times, I think you'll agree, when false courage is better than no courage at all. At least, tomorrow morning the soldier will wake up alive in his forest hideout rather than lie cut down like a barley stalk on a senseless, soon-to-be-forgotten battlefield.

"And before Christmas, our other man will be walking down the aisle with the girl he adores, instead of weeping alone in an empty room while she weds another, less worthy suitor."

Gracie loved all this drama. It was like watching TV. Thanks to the fairy, there were even beer commercials.

"Courage is where you find it. Having said that, I must admit that bravery that comes from a bottle—or from a book or a sermon, for that matter—lacks the full strength and purity of bravery that comes straight from the heart. Your bravery came from your heart, Gracie. I was significantly impressed."

"Hi de...," Gracie began, but before she could get the "ho" out, the Beer Fairy interrupted.

"I want you to promise me that you'll always be this brave, that when exploiters disguised as public servants offer you protection from puffed-up dangers, you'll turn your back and skip away. Promise me you won't be afraid of travel, of people different than yourself, of spiders, bats, bullies, dentists, attorneys, peer pressure, bad taste, social disapproval, insecurity, Sugar Elves...."

"Why would Sugar Elfs...?"

"Never mind. That you won't quake before old men with titles, and most especially, that you'll never be afraid to love, not even when there's a chance you aren't being loved in return."

Gracie nodded in tentative agreement. "Are you a phil... a phil... a philockerfer?" she asked, obviously thinking of Uncle Moe.

Her tiny teacher laughed. "A philosopher? Not me, kiddo. I'm just your ordinary universal Beer Fairy."

"But," said Gracie, frowning about two wrinkles' worth, "they're drinking lots of beer down there in… in Pimple-on-Toast. Why aren't you down there with them?"

"I am."

Anticipating Gracie's confusion, the fairy let her fret a moment before going on to say, "I'm very much present at that village festival, and I'm at another harvest festival downriver at Poop-on-Shingle. I'm in a dozen rowdy taverns in Alaska, a hundred Irish pubs, a tailgate party in Ohio, a factory opening in Korea, et cetera, et cetera; and I'm also completely and totally here with you. That's the way it is with my kind. I can be many places at once. And now, I—and you—need to be somewhere else."

Deftly, she slid her wand between Gracie's fingers, and it was *poof* time again.

The next thing Gracie knew, she was lying on her bed at home. She stared almost in wonder at the familiar surroundings. Oddly enough, her Hello Kitty ticktock clock indicated that no more than ten or twelve minutes had passed since she'd looked at it last. The pool of upchuck on the carpet was still shiny and bright.

No, it hadn't been a dream, in case that's what you're thinking. The Beer Fairy was right there with Gracie, perched on her chest. "Promise me something else," the fairy said. "You mustn't drink beer again until you're at least eighteen. And you must never, ever drink and drive."

The idea of herself behind the wheel of a car struck the kindergartner as so comical she giggled out loud. She agreed, nonetheless, and as she was giving her promise, they heard footsteps on the stairs.

"I'm blowing this pop stand!" exclaimed the Beer Fairy. She flew up to whisper something in Gracie's ear, then in a flash (or, rather, a *poof*), she shot toward the ceiling and vanished.

Mrs. Perkel was at the door. "Gracie, are you in there? What happened to your cake? What's that awful smell?"

18

Well, boys and girls, assuming you've been paying attention, you now know everything you'll ever need or want to know about the world's most popular adult beverage. True, we didn't examine from a scientific standpoint the precise physical effects the consumption of beer has on the brain, the belly, and the liver. Should you crave such information you can always consult your pediatrician—although don't be surprised if he gives you a funny look. He's likely to look at you strangely even if he's Irish.

There is one other thing. Should you have nothing better to do than to delve further into the origins of beer, you'll come across some historians who contend that beer was invented in Sumer, the present-day country of Iraq, centuries before it was first brewed in Egypt. The Beer Fairy concedes that the Sumerians did, indeed, ferment a kind of grain drink, but that it would be stretching the point to actually call the slop beer. The Beer Fairy ought to know.

Okay, that's that. We've reached the bottom of the keg, so to speak. Let's bid one another good-bye and good luck. Ciao, babies. You, too, Grandpa. Go forth with gusto.

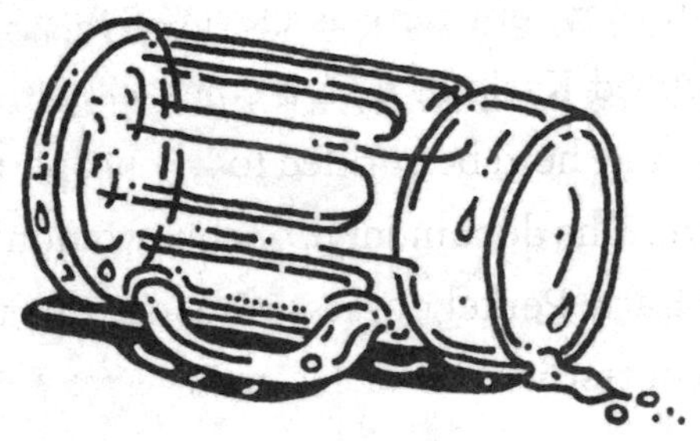

Oh, by the way, in case any among you are interested in what happened to Gracie Perkel, it's sad to report that in the days, weeks, and months following her birthday escapades her woes did not diminish nor her home life improve.

Upon her daddy's return from Arizona, he and her mommy engaged in a vicious, tongue-smoking, brain-skinning, milk-souring argument. They continued to fight like that, off and on, until deep into December. Two days before Christmas, they called their daughter into the den, set her down, and told her they were getting a divorce.

No child wants to hear that her parents are divorcing, but Gracie took it fairly well. She had, if you recall, made a promise to maintain a brave heart. She only cried once or twice. Maybe three times.

Matters got worse. Charlie Perkel was not a particularly successful attorney, but he was clever. Before their wedding, he had convinced Karla to sign a contract stating that should they ever divorce, he'd be entitled to any properties they might jointly acquire. The document probably wouldn't have held up in court, but Karla Perkel possessed neither the money nor the stomach to contest it. She and Gracie were forced to vacate their home.

Since she'd dropped out of college in her sophomore year to get married (she'd been an honor-roll major in social studies), Karla lacked the proper education or experience for rewarding employment. She took a part-time job in a doughnut shop, and with her minimum-wage salary, food stamps, and—when he remembered to send it—Mr. Perkel's monthly child-support payment, mother and daughter moved into a vermin-gnawed one-bedroom apartment on a sketchy street in White Center, a ticky-tacky, blue-collar Seattle neighborhood noted for the size of its rats, the aroma of its cooking grease, and the frequency of its gunfire.

They couldn't afford cable, so Gracie went back to *Finding Nemo*, watching the video so many times she surely could have qualified for a mention in *Guinness World Records* (a book, incidentally, that owed its existence to… beer).

One Saturday afternoon, Gracie awoke from a nap to discover her mother sitting at the kitchen table sipping a cheap brand of beer from a can. There were two or three empty cans on the tabletop in front of her.

Gracie frowned. Like a pea-size groundhog, a single drop abruptly poked its bald head out of her left tear hole and seemed to peer around for a moment, although due to the dim light in the room it could not have seen its shadow. With a blink, she shooed it away, but having only duct for cover, it popped right back up again.

Except for an occasional glass of wine, Gracie had never known her mother to touch alcohol. "Mo-Mo-Mommy," she began, stuttering as if she were back in that chilly conditioning room at the brewery. "Please don't." She paused, searching for the right words.

"Beer's nice for being glad and dizzy and sometimes for the Mystery and stuff, but the happy that comes out of a beer can is not like the real happy you got to make in your heart." She paused again. "When the beer's done working, you'll only feel badder."

It was Karla's turn to entertain a teardrop. She pushed her chair away from the table and rose to give her small daughter a hug. "I swear, Grace Olivia Perkel, sometimes you almost scare me, you're so… so wise. Where on Earth did you learn to give advice like that?" She supposed it was the influence of the "ol' philosopher," though she couldn't conceive of the likes of Moe Babbano having anything negative to say about beer. Or if he did, it wouldn't be in plain American television English that people could actually comprehend. "Where did you ever learn…?"

"From a fairy," Gracie chirped, just blurting it out—and instantly regretting it, wishing she could stuff the syllables back in her mouth.

The mother smiled. "A fairy, huh? Despite everything, you've certainly not lost your imagination." She walked to the sink, hesitated, took one last swallow, and poured the remaining beer down the drain. "Well, maybe you and I can imagine we're going to share a pint of vanilla Häagen-Dazs for our dinner tonight."

"Rocky road," muttered Gracie.

As it was, they dined on buttered noodles that evening, and there was no dessert.

Eventually, the ol' philosopher himself got wind of their situation. At once, he invited them to come live with him and Dr. Proust in Costa Rica. Karla politely declined. There quickly followed a second invitation. Karla declined again. Ah, but Gracie: she pleaded and pleaded and pleaded; pleaded so long, so hard, so persistently, so sweetly, so annoyingly, that she could have landed in the Guinness record book for pleading, as well.

Finally, with the arrival of a third invitation that included plane tickets, her poor mother caved in. On a Tuesday near the middle of summer, the pair found themselves on a flight jetting south-southeastward: past Texas, past Mexico, past Nicaragua, down to far Costa Rica. If they flew over Pimple-on-Chin, Gracie didn't recognize it.

Travel-weary, but excited (well, Gracie, at least, was excited), they were welcomed to a roomy, colonial-style house in between the jungle and the sea. Surrounded by coconut palms, the house had a white stucco facade, a red-tile roof, and heavy brown shutters to hold back hurricane winds and the tropical sun. There were ceiling fans that kept mosquitoes off-balance and lulled nappers to sleep.

Outdoors, the air seemed as thick and sweet as chocolate cake batter; flavored by spice plants, scented with blossoms, stirred by the wings of neon-feathered birds, purplish bats, and butterflies the size of table-tennis paddles. At first, the Seattle girl took offense at the heat. She actually missed the drizzle—or did she miss that "Other" that lay between the mist and the murk? (Between the chop and the suey?)

It was always cool and dim in the house, however. Gracie especially liked padding barefoot along the ceramic tile floors. She would have relished walking around birth-naked, but there were too many eyes. From the walls of every room small lizards constantly monitored human activities, and, moreover, Uncle Moe had acquired a parrot. A fat, cherry-lemonade-colored bird, it commanded a perch in the courtyard, occasionally squawking long sentences in Spanish. Within a week, Gracie had taught it to say "hi de ho." The parrot seemed to enjoy the phrase as much as Gracie, uttering it with such frequency it just about drove everybody nuts.

While her departure had little or nothing to do with the hi-de-hoing parrot, shortly after Gracie and her mom moved in, Madeline Proust moved out. Her hot romance with Moe Babbano had cooled off (as, kids, hot romances often do), and she'd come to miss the tortured feet of Seattle. Before departing, she generously offered to sign over the house to Moe. On one condition: he had to shave off his mustache. She claimed it was for the benefit of society at large, since she, personally, would no longer be exposed to it.

The shaving ceremony was held in the courtyard. Pausing periodically to pronounce lines in Latin that nobody understood, Moe took an hour to scrape the melancholy growth, that electrocuted chickadee, off of his upper lip. "It's the end of an era," he said solemnly. "Mustaches such as this come around once in a generation." The rest of the party applauded when the terminated whiskers, laid out elaborately in a coconut shell, were buried beneath a jasmine bush.

With Dr. Proust gone and autumn on the way, homeschooling began in earnest for Gracie. Her mother taught her simple arithmetic and how to read and write in English. Uncle Moe instructed her in Spanish vocabulary, in philosophy, poetry, cool jazz, how the stars and planets got their names, and other subjects which, to her mind if not to his, had a hint of the Mystery about them.

Gracie taught her uncle something, as well. Although Imperial beer was widely available, and the ol' Moester consumed his share of it (he never once offered Gracie a sip, nor did she request one), he decided to brew some beer of his own. He purchased a sack of malted barley and set about cooking and fermenting it in a shack behind the house. Were it not for Gracie, who offered him helpful tips along the way, he might not have succeeded. Moe was astonished at her knowledge of brewing techniques.

"How do you know all this?" he demanded. Gracie merely shrugged. It did occur to her that of all people, her Uncle Moe would have accepted, understood, maybe even personally related, but when it came to her adventure with the Beer Fairy, her lips were forever zipped. (Should you travel to Costa Rica one of these days and run into a spunky little blonde with guitar-blue eyes, don't start bugging her about pixies, *poofs*, and pilsners, she'll just turn her back and skip away.)

For brewing, Moe used collected rainwater from a barrel. The water had run off of the shack's tar paper roof. As a result, the beer he produced was black as night and had some kind of green moss growing on its surface. Whether it would have pleased the palate of vinegar eels is hard to say, but Moe declared it quite tasty. On the evenings when he drank it, he invariably saw UFOs.

If you quizzed her, Gracie would have answered that her life in Costa Rica was pretty good. At times, it came close to being glad and dizzy. For her seventh birthday (yes, a whole year had elapsed since fateful Number 6), she failed once again to receive a pink cell phone, and it appeared that she was destined to go through life without one. She didn't get that puppy, either. But she did get a monkey.

She named the monkey Häagen-Dazs, but since no one present, not even the heavily educated Moe Babbano, could spell Häagen-Dazs, she soon changed its name to Hiccup. The two became rapidly inseparable. At last, the only child had a dance partner.

Out on the veranda, Gracie and Hiccup would perform cheerfully wild boogaloos, largely of Gracie's invention, although the monkey did contribute routines of its own. Children from the area would gather to watch. Normally bashful, they'd sometimes break into giggle fits and shy applause. They'd bring gifts of coffee beans and bananas. Usually, they'd scatter and hide behind trees whenever Uncle Moe ventured out onto the veranda to join in on bongo drums, hiding even though Moe wasn't nearly as funny looking now that his facial hair had gone to mustache heaven. Or mustache hell.

Despite schooling and monkeyshines and trips to the beach, their time passed slowly in the tropics, passing in harmony with the creaky old wooden ceiling fans. Then something momentous occurred; something strange, dramatic, and completely unexpected. Karla and Moe fell in love.

Technically speaking, that isn't entirely accurate. Karla and Moe didn't fall in love, Karla and Moe discovered that they'd been secretly in love all along, had been secretly in love for years, had been in love so secretly that they'd kept the secret even from themselves, kept it locked away in the deep velvet vaults of their hearts. Now some force must have jimmied the locks.

(If somebody ever calls you a "weirdo" or a "nut job," you should consider the possibility that he or she has a secret crush on you.)

In any event, on the eve of the U.S. Thanksgiving holiday, Gracie's mommy and uncle were married at a little thatched-roof shrine in the jungle. The groom wore his white suit, which had turned rather yellow from age, and read aloud a poem by a crazy dead Frenchman. The bride, who'd imprisoned her pretty feet in tight shoes for years, stood beaming in floppy straw sandals. Hiccup the monkey attended in one of Gracie's old dresses; the parrot, from the rear of the hut, squawked "hi de ho" incessantly; and, at the appropriate moment, Gracie squealed with such joy she nearly peed in her pants.

So, now you know. There they were. And did they live happily ever after? No, nobody ever does—at least not totally. But whenever Karla was blindsided by bad days, as most of us are from time to time, she'd make a point of refusing to take them too seriously, and that, dear reader, is the next best thing to everlasting happiness.

By the most narrow of margins, Costa Rica had elected a conservative president, and though Moe was worried that the enlightened little nation would now be led down the path of relentless, sordid moneygrubbing (which seems to be the principal activity of conservative societies everywhere), he was too wise to let politics spoil his ongoing honeymoon with Karla and with life.

For her part, on those rare occasions when her customary high spirits showed signs of taking a dive, Gracie, sooner or later, would remind herself of the parting words the Beer Fairy had whispered in her ear.

"We'll meet again someday," the Beer Fairy had prophesied.

"The ordinary world is only the foam on top of the real world, the deeper world—and someday you and I will meet again."

ACKNOWLEDGEMENTS

When Uncle Moe refers to Gracie's "monkey dance of life" he's riffing on a line from Jack Kerouac. I'd love to pour Jack's ghost a beer—although in life he seemed to prefer cheap red wine.

Preferences aside, I'm here to roll out a barrel of gratitude to the editorial brain trust on East 53rd Street, most particularly Daniel Halpern, Abigail Holstein, and the legendary David Hershey (with his special knowledge of the interpenetration of realities); a second keg of thanks to Barb Bersche and the talented folks at McSweeney's; and yet another to the artist Leslie LePere, for whom every pencil, every pen is a baton, a wand, a bottle rocket, a customized '51 Mercury he drives to town on Saturday nights.

Let me also lift a convivial mug to E. Jean Carroll, Phoebe Larmore, Alexa Robbins, David McCumber, Russ Reising, and Lee Frederick, among a handful of friends who assured me I could when other parties were warning that I couldn't or shouldn't, or wouldn't bloody dare.

—T.R.

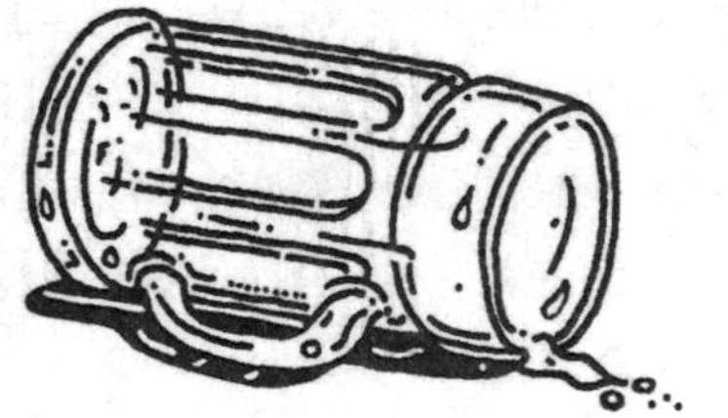